The Best of
Weird Tales: 1923

Other Books from Bleak House

THE BEST OF WEIRD TALES: 1924
(forthcoming)

THE EARTH IS MADE OF STARDUST . . .
The Collected Short Stories of Morgan Llywelyn
(forthcoming)

The Best of
Weird Tales: 1923

Selected and Edited by
Marvin Kaye
& John Gregory Betancourt

Cover illustration by
Stephen Fabian

BLEAK☠HOUSE
Berkeley Heights, NJ • 1997

Contents

Back to the Haunting Past

I was born the same year Orson Welles panicked America. By the time I was old enough to know about events outside the Philadelphia slum block I lived in, World War II was under way and most of my uncles and cousins were in the army or the navy. It was a frightening time for an impressionable child. On the one hand, I yearned for gentler myths than war, yet like most children, my imagination also craved stories of danger and terror, provided they culminated in victory by moral courage, fortitude and wit, those 1940s "American" virtues practiced by such heroes as Captains Marvel and Midnight, Spy Smasher, Tom Mix and especially those three intrepid musketeers of radio who rushed in where Indiana Jones might fear to tread, Carlton E. Morse's mystery-loving Jack, Doc and Reggie.

Radio and the movie theatre across the street enthralled me, but there was another powerful stimulant in our "West Philly" household at 429 North 60th Street, a pulp magazine with eerie covers and stories that, long before I had the skill or patience to read them, fired my imagination, tales with shivery titles like "The Golden Goblins," "Lords of the Ghostlands," "Let's Play Poison" or "The Music-Box from Hell"—*Weird Tales*, which (with minimal hyperbole) its publishers styled "The Unique Magazine."

I suppose it was my father who bought *Weird Tales*, though I never actually saw him holding or reading an issue. Copies just showed up from time to time till my mother tossed them out. My relatives and teachers regarded such literature as worthless, but I knew better. Throughout its long, interrupted history from 1923 to the present, *Weird Tales* has consistently presented the best (and worst) genre literature, from grisly murder stories through dark and light fantasy to occasional science-fiction, and has continued to feature a host of the finest category and "mainstream" writers living and dead.

As I grew up, I browsed *Weird Tales* whenever I could, though I seldom could afford the price of a copy. I did manage to spend a large chunk of allowance (thirty-five cents!) on the September 1954 *Weird Tales*, not realizing it would be the last issue to be published until Leo Margulies revived "The Unique Magazine" nineteen years later.

The magazine died and came back to life so often that when I did a *Weird Tales* commemorative anthology in 1988 for the Doubleday Book and Music Clubs, I dubbed it "The Magazine That Never Dies." The story of *Weird Tales*'s many incarnations and reincarnations appears in brief in my earlier collection, and in considerably greater detail in Bob Weinberg's essential history-appreciation, *The Weird Tales Story*, which Bleak House hopes to reissue in the near future.

In *Weird Tales, the Magazine that Never Dies*, I offered an assortment of forty-five selections from the magazine's seven distinct editor/publisherships. In this generous-sized volume, I included selections by many of *Weird Tales*'s popular contributors, including such important fantasists as, for example, Robert Bloch, Ray Bradbury, Fredric Brown. Hugh B. Cave, L. Sprague de Camp & Fletcher Pratt, August Derleth, Robert E. Howard, Fritz Leiber, Jr., Frank Belknap Long, H. P. Lovecraft, Richard Matheson, Seabury Quinn, Clark Ashton Smith and Theodore Sturgeon, as well as interesting pieces by other less-familiar authors . . . yet I was then and am now keenly aware of how much "good stuff" I reluctantly had to omit.

As a collector, I've always wanted to own a complete run of *Weird Tales* (I'm halfway there). Thus, I heartily endorsed the suggestion of my friend and associate John Betancourt to launch Bleak House with a selection drawn from the first year of "The Unique Magazine" which, if successful, will be followed by similar year-by-year anthologies.

With patience, luck and the generous assistance of several collectors, notably Graham Holroyd, Bob Madle, Bob Weinberg, and Jon White, I tracked down and read every issue of *Weird Tales* published in 1923 and discovered that though "The Unique Magazine" did not hit its stride for several months, more good fiction appeared in the opening year than I'd expected to find. My initial fear that there wouldn't be enough first-rate material to fill a modest-sized volume not only proved unfounded, but instead, I again was faced with the frustrating task of eliminating worthwhile stories, some because they were too long, some by authors already represented (each writer was restricted to a single entry).

The thirteen tales I chose represent some of the best—and often, some of the least-known—tales to appear in the first year of "The

Unique Magazine." At least one piece from each issue has been included. Month-by-month prefatory rubrics provide further comment.

Now, to paraphrase a popular rock group, welcome back, my friends, to the magazine that never ends: *Weird Tales, the Beginning!*

—Marvin Kaye
New York 1995

MARCH 1923

In 1922, Jacob C. Henneberger, of Lancaster, Pennsylvania, and John Lansinger created Rural Publications, Inc., to publish three magazines, *Mystery Stories*, *Real Detective Tales* and *Weird Tales*.

The first issue of *Weird Tales*, edited by Edwin Baird, appeared in March, 1923, ran 192 pages, measured 6" by 9", cost a quarter, and had a cover by R. R. Epperly illustrating Anthony M. Rud's "Ooze." The editorial column was dubbed "The Eyrie." One of Baird's staff, Otis Adelbert Kline, contributed "The Thing of a Thousand Shapes," first of a long series of serials to appear subsequently in *Weird Tales*. Another editor, Chicago music critic Farnsworth Wright, wrote "The Closing Hand," the first of five stories he penned for the magazine in 1923. The following year, Wright assumed editorship and fashioned *Weird Tales* into America's most important genre magazine.

Volume I, Number 1 contains twenty-six stories that run the gamut from plain-awful through competent but predictable to a modest number of well-written, memorably gruesome tales. Kline's novella has been reprinted elsewhere, as has been Hamilton Craigie's "The Chain" and Rud's title story, but I thought the latter pair poorly written and also was disappointed with "Hark! The Rattle!" a purple exercise by Joel Townsley Rogers, who produced far better work in The Red Right Hand, featured in the 1950s in Dell's Great Mystery Library series. The first issue's lead-off story by Julian Kilman is excellent (see Afterword), but he is represented later in this volume, so I chose, instead, Orville R. Emerson's horrific "The Grave" and Herbert J. Mangham's "The Basket," a hauntingly understated vignette that reminds me of the bleak existential fiction of Albert Camus.

The Grave

ORVILLE R. EMERSON

The end of this story was first brought to my attention when Fromwiller returned from his trip to Mount Kemmel, with a very strange tale to tell, indeed, and one extremely hard to believe. But I believed it enough to go back to the Mount with "From" to see if we could discover anything more. And after digging for a while at the place where "From's" story began, we made our way into an old dugout that had been caved in, or at least where all the entrances had been filled with dirt, and there we found, written on German correspondence paper, a terrible story.

We found the story on Christmas Day, 1918, while making the trip in the colonel's machine from Watou, in Flanders, where our regiment was stationed. Of course, you have heard of Mount Kemmel in Flanders; more than once it figured in the newspaper reports as it changed hands during some of the fiercest fighting of the war. And when the Germans were finally driven from this point of vantage, in October 1918, a retreat was started which did not end until it became a race to see who could get into Germany first.

The advance was so fast that the victorious British and French forces had no time to bury their dead, and, terrible as it may seem to those who have not seen it, in December of that year one could see the rotting corpses of the unburied dead scattered here and there over the top of Mount Kemmel. It was a place of ghastly sights and sickening odors. And it was there that we found this tale.

With the chaplain's help, we translated the story, which follows:

"For two weeks I have been buried alive! For two weeks I have not seen daylight, nor heard the sound of another person's voice. Unless I can find something to do, besides this everlasting digging, I shall go mad. So I shall write. As long as my candles last, I will pass part of the time each day in setting down on paper my experiences.

"Not that I need to do this in order to remember them. God knows that when I get out, the first thing I shall do will be to try to forget them! But if I should *not* get out . . . !

"I am an Ober-lieutenant in the Imperial German Army. Two weeks ago my regiment was holding Mount Kemmel in Flanders. We were surrounded on three sides, and subjected to a terrific artillery fire, but on account of the commanding position we were ordered to hold the Mount to the last man. Our engineers, however, had made things very comfortable. Numerous deep dugouts had been constructed, and in them we were comparatively safe from shellfire.

"Many of these had been connected by passageways so that there was a regular little underground city, and the majority of the garrison never left the protection of the dugouts. But even under these conditions our casualties were heavy. Lookouts had to be maintained above ground, and once in a while a direct hit by one of the huge railway guns would even destroy some of the dugouts.

"A little over two weeks ago—I can't be sure, because I have lost track of the exact number of days—the usual shelling was increased a hundred fold. With about twenty others, I was sleeping in one of the shallower dugouts. The tremendous increase in shelling awakened me with a start, and my first impulse was to go at once into a deeper dugout, which was connected to the one I was in by an underground passageway.

"It was a smaller dugout, built a few feet lower than the one I was in. It had been used as a sort of a storeroom and no one was supposed to sleep there. But it seemed safer to me, and, alone, I crept into it. A thousand times since I have wished I had taken another man with me. But my chances for doing it were soon gone.

"I had hardly entered the smaller dugout when there was a tremendous explosion behind me. The ground shook as if a mine had exploded below us. Whether that was indeed the case, or whether some extra large caliber explosive shell had struck the dugout behind me, I never knew.

"After the shock of the explosion had passed, I went back to the passageway. When about halfway along it, I found the timbers above had fallen, allowing the earth to settle, and my way was effectually blocked.

"So I returned to the dugout and waited alone through several hours of terrific shelling. The only other entrance to the dugout I was in was the main entrance from the trench above, and all those who had been above ground had gone into dugouts long before this. So I could not expect anyone to enter while the shelling continued; and when it ceased there would surely be an attack.

"As I did not want to be killed by a grenade thrown down the entrance, I remained awake in order to rush out at the first signs of cessation of the bombardment and join what comrades there might be left on the hill.

"After about six hours of the heavy bombardment, all sound above ground seemed to cease. Five minutes went by, then ten; surely the attack was coming. I rushed to the stairway leading out to the air. I took a couple of strides up the stairs. There was a blinding flash and a deafening explosion.

"I felt myself falling. Then darkness swallowed everything.

How long I lay unconscious in the dugout I never knew.

"But after what seemed like a long time, I practically grew conscious of a dull ache in my left arm. I could not move it. I opened my eyes and found only darkness. I felt pain and a stiffness all over my body.

"Slowly I rose, struck a match, found a candle and lit it and looked at my watch. It had stopped. I did not know how long I had remained there unconscious. All noise of bombardment had ceased. I stood and listened for some time, but could hear no sound of any kind.

"My gaze fell on the stairway entrance. I started in alarm. The end of the dugout, where the entrance was, was half filled with dirt.

"I went over and looked closer. The entrance was completely filled with dirt at the bottom, and no light of any kind could be seen from above. I went to the passageway to the other dugout, although I remembered it had caved in. I examined the fallen timbers closely. Between two of them I could feel a slight movement of air. Here was an opening to the outside world.

"I tried to move the timbers, as well as I could with one arm, only to precipitate a small avalanche of dirt which filled the crack. Quickly I dug at the dirt until again I could feel the movement of air. This might be the only place where I could obtain fresh air.

"I was convinced that it would take some little work to open up either of the passageways, and I began to feel hungry. Luckily, there was a good supply of canned foods and hard bread, for the officers had kept their rations stored in this dugout. I also found a keg of water and about a dozen bottles of wine, which I discovered to be very good. After I had relieved my appetite and finished one of the bottles of wine, I felt sleepy and, although my left arm pained me considerably, I soon dropped off to sleep.

"The time I have allowed myself for writing is up, so I will stop for today. After I have performed my daily task of digging tomorrow, I shall again write. Already my mind feels easier. Surely help will come soon. At any rate, within two more weeks I shall have liberated myself. Already I am halfway up the stairs. And my rations will last that long. I have divided them so they will.

"Yesterday I did not feel like writing after I finished my digging. My arm pained me considerably. I guess I used it too much.

"But today I was more careful with it, and it feels better. And I am worried again. Twice today big piles of earth caved in, where the timbers above were loose, and each time as much dirt fell into the passageway as I can remove in a day. Two days more before I can count on getting out by myself.

"The rations will have to be stretched out some more. The daily amount is already pretty small. But I shall go on with my account.

"From the time I became conscious I started my watch, and since then I have kept track of the days. On the second day I took stock of the food, water, wood, matches, candles, etc., and found a plentiful supply for two weeks at least. At that time I did not look forward to a stay of more than a few days in my prison.

"Either the enemy or ourselves will occupy the hill, I told myself, because it is such an important position. And whoever now holds the hill will be compelled to dig in deeply in order to hold it.

"So to my mind it was only a matter of a few days until either the entrance or the passageway would be cleared, and my only doubts were as to whether it would be friends or enemies that would discover me. My arm felt better, although I could not use it much, and so I spent the day in reading an old newspaper which I found among the food supplies, and in waiting for help to come. What a fool I was! If I had only worked from the start, I would be just that many days nearer deliverance.

"On the third day I was annoyed by water, which began dripping from the roof and seeping in at the sides of the dugout. I cursed that muddy water, then, as I have often cursed such dugout nuisances before, but it may be that I shall yet bless that water and it shall save my life.

"But it certainly made things uncomfortable; so I spent the day in moving my bunk, food and water supplies, candles, etc., up into the passageway. For a space of about ten feet it was unobstructed, and, being slightly higher than the dugout, was dryer and more comfortable. Besides, the air came in through the crack between the timbers, and I thought maybe the rats wouldn't bother me so much at night. Again I spent the balance of the day simply in waiting for help.

"It was not until well into the fourth day that I really began to feel uneasy. It suddenly became impressed on my consciousness that I had not heard the sound of a gun, or felt the earth shake from the force of a concussion, since the fatal shell that had filled the entrance. What was the meaning of the silence? Why did I hear no sounds of fighting? It was as still as the grave.

"What a horrible death to die! Buried alive! A panic of fear swept over me. But my will and reason reasserted itself. In time, I should be able to dig myself out on my own efforts.

"So although I could not use my left arm as yet, I spent the rest of that day and all of the two following days in digging dirt from the entrance and carrying it back into the far corner of the dugout.

"On the seventh day after regaining consciousness I was tired and stiff from my unwanted exertions of the three previous days. I could see by this time that it was a matter of weeks—two or three, at least—before I could hope to liberate myself. I might be rescued at an earlier date, but without outside aid, it would take probably three more weeks of labor before I could dig my way out.

"Already dirt had caved in from the top, where the timbers had sprung apart, and I could repair the damage to the roof of the stairway only in a crude way with one arm. But my left arm was much better. With a day's rest, I would be able to use it pretty well. Besides, I must conserve my energy. So I spent the seventh day in rest and prayer for my speedy release from a living grave.

"I also reapportioned my food on the basis of three more weeks. It made the daily portions pretty small, especially as the digging was strenuous work. There was a large supply of candles, so that I had plenty of light for my work. But the supply of water bothered me. Almost half of the small keg was gone in the first week. I decided to drink only once a day.

"The following six days were all days of feverish labor, light eating and even lighter drinking. But, despite all my efforts, only a quarter of the keg was left at the end of two weeks. And the horror of the situation grew on me. My imagination would not be quiet. I would picture to myself the agonies to come, when I would have even less food and water than at present. My mind would run on and on—to death by starvation—to the finding of my emaciated body by those who would eventually open up the dugout—even to their attempts to reconstruct the story of my end.

"And, adding to my physical discomfort, were the swarming vermin infesting the dugout and my person. A month had gone by since I had had a bath, and I could not now spare a drop of water even to wash my face. The rats had become so bold that I had to leave a candle burning all night in order to protect myself in my sleep.

"Partly to relieve my mind, I started to write this tale of my experiences. It did act as a relief at first, but now, as I read it over, the growing terror of this awful place grips me. I would cease writing, but some impluse urges me to write each day.

***

"Three weeks have passed since I was buried in this living tomb.

"Today I drank the last drop of water in the keg. There is a pool of stagnant water on the dugout floor—dirty, slimy and alive with vermin—always standing there, fed by drippings from the roof. As yet I cannot bring myself to touch it.

"Today I divided up my food supply for another week. God knows the portions were already small enough! But there have been so many cave-ins recently that I can never finish clearing the entrance in another week.

"Sometimes I feel that I shall never clear it. But I *must*! I can never bear to die here. I must will myself to escape, and *I shall escape*!

"Did not the captain often say that the will to win was half the victory? I shall rest no more. Every waking hour must be spent in removing the treacherous dirt.

"Even my writing must cease.

"Oh God! I am afraid, *afraid*!

"I must write to relieve my mind. Last night I went to sleep at nine by my watch. At twelve I woke to find myself in the dark, frantically digging with my bare hands at the hard sides of the dugout. After some trouble I found a candle and lit it.

"The whole dugout was upset. My food supplies were lying in the mud. The box of candles had been spilled. My fingernails were broken and bloody from clawing at the ground.

"The realization dawned upon me that I had been out of my head. And then came the fear—dark, raging, fear—fear of insanity. I have been drinking the stagnant water from the floor for days. I do not know how many.

"I have only about one meal left, but I must save it.

"I had a meal today. For three days I have been without food.

"But today I caught one of the rats that infest the place. He was a big one, too. Gave me a bad bite, but I killed him. I feel lots better today. Have had some bad dreams lately, but they don't bother me now.

"That rat was tough, though. Think I'll finish this digging and go back to my regiment in a day or two.

"Heaven have mercy! I must be out of my head half the time now.

"I have absolutely no recollection of having written that last entry. And I feel feverish and weak.

"If I had my strength, I think I could finish clearing the entrance in a day or two. But I can only work a short time at a stretch.

"I am beginning to give up hope.

"Wild spells come on me oftener now. I awake tired out from exertions, which I cannot remember.

"Bones of rats, picked clean, are scattered about, yet I do not remember eating them. In my lucid moments I don't seem to be able to catch them, for they are too wary and I am too weak.

"I get some relief by chewing the candles, but I dare not eat them all. I am afraid of the dark, I am afraid of the rats, but worst of all is the hideous fear of myself.

"My mind is breaking down. I must escape soon, or I will be little better than a wild animal. Oh, God, send help! I am going mad!

"Terror, desperation, despair—is this the end?

"For a long time I have been resting.

"I have had a brilliant idea. Rest brings back strength. The longer a person rests the stronger they should get. I have been resting a long time now. Weeks or months, I don't know which. So I must be very strong. I feel strong. My fever has left me. So listen! There is only a little dirt left in the entrance way. I am going out and crawl through it. Just like a mole. Right out into the sunlight. I feel much stronger than a mole. So this is the end of my little tale. A sad tale, but one with a happy ending. Sunlight! A very happy ending."

And that was the end of the manuscript. There only remains to tell Fromwillwer's tale.

At first I didn't believe it. But now I do. I shall put it down, though, just as Fromwiller told it to me, and you can take it or leave it as you choose.

"Soon after we were billeted at Watou," said Fromwiller, "I decided to go out and see Mount Kemmel. I had heard that things were rather gruesome out there, but I was really not prepared for the conditions that I found. I had seen unburied dead around Roulers and in the Argonne, but it had been almost two months since the fighting on Mount Kemmel and there were still many unburied dead. But there was another thing that I had never seen, and that was the *buried living*!

"As I came up to the highest point of the Mount, I was attracted by a movement of loose dirt on the edge of a huge shell hole. The dirt seemed to be falling in to a common center, as if the dirt below was being removed. As I watched, suddenly I was horrified to see a long, skinny human arm emerge from the ground.

"It disappeared, drawing back some of the earth with it. There was a movement of dirt over a larger area, and the arm reappeared, together with a man's head and shoulders. He pulled himself up out of the very ground, as it seemed, shook the dirt from his body like a huge, gaunt dog, and stood erect. I never want to see such another creature!

"Hardly a strip of clothing was visible, and, what little there was, was so torn and dirty that it was impossible to tell what kind it had been. The skin was drawn tightly over the bones, and there was a vacant stare in the protruding eyes. It looked like a corpse that had lain in the grave a long time.

"This apparition looked directly at me, and yet did not appear to see me. He looked as if the light bothered him. I spoke, and a look of fear came over his face. He seemed filled with terror.

"I stepped toward him, shaking loose a piece of barbed wire which had caught in my puttees. Quick as a flash, he turned and started to run from me.

"For a second I was too astonished to move. Then I started to follow him. In a straight line he ran, looking neither to the right or left. Directly ahead of him was a deep and wide trench. He was running straight toward it. Suddenly it dawned on me that he did not see it.

"I called out, but it seemed to terrify him all the more, and with one last lunge he stepped into the trench and fell. I heard his body strike the other side of the trench anf fall with a splash into the water at the bottom.

"I followed and looked down into the trench. There he lay, with his head bent back in such a position that I was sure his neck was broken. He was half in and half out of the water, and as I looked at him I could scarcely believe what I had seen. Surely he looked as if he had been dead as long as some of the other corpses, scattered over the hillside. I turned and left him as he was.

"Buried while living, I left him unburied when dead."

The Basket

HERBERT J. MANGHAM

Mrs. Buhler told him at first that she had no vacancies, but as he started away she thought of the little room in the basement.

He turned back at her call.

"I have got a room, too," she said, "but it's a very small one and in the basement. I can make you a reasonable price, though, if you'd care to look at it."

The room was a problem. She always hesitated to show it to people, because so often they seemed insulted at her suggestion that they would be satisfied with such humble surroundings. If she gave it to the first applicant, he would likely be a disreputable character who might detract from the respectability of the house, and she would have to face the embarrassment of getting rid of him. So she was content for weeks at a time to do without the pittance the room brought her.

"How much is it?" asked the man.

"Seven dollars a month."

"Let me see it."

She called her husband to take her place at the desk, picked up a bunch of keys and led the way to the rear of the basement. The room was a narrow cell, whose one window was slightly below the level of a tiny, bare back yard, closed in by a board fence.

A tottering oak dresser was pushed up close to the window, and a small square table, holding a pitcher and washbowl, was standing beside it. An iron single-bed against the opposite wall left barely enough space for one straight-backed chair and a narrow path from the door to the window. A curtain, hanging across one corner, and a couple of hooks in the wall provided a substitute for a closet.

"You can have the use of the bathroom on the first floor," said Mrs. Buhler. "There is no steam heat in the basement, but I will give you an oil stove to use if you want it. The oil won't cost you very much. Of course, it never gets real cold in San Francisco, but when the fogs come in off the bay you ought to have something to take the chill off the room."

"I'll take it."

The man pulled out a small roll of money and counted off seven one-dollar bills.

"You must be from the East," remarked Mrs. Buhler, smiling at the paper money.

"Yes."

Mrs. Buhler, looking at his pale hair and eyes and wan mustache, never thought of asking for references. He seemed as incapable of mischief as a retired fire horse, munching his grass and dreaming of past adventures.

He told her that his name was Dave Scannon.

And that was all the information he ever volunteered to anybody in the rooming-house.

An hour later he moved in. By carrying in one suitcase and transferring its contents to the dresser drawers he was installed.

The other roomers scarcely noticed his advent. He always walked straight across the little lobby without looking directly at anyone, never stopping except to pay his rent, which he did promptly on the fifth of every month.

He did not leave his key at the desk when he went out, as was the custom of the house, but carried it in his pocket. The chambermaid never touched his room. At his request she gave him a broom, and every Sunday morning she left towels, sheets and a pillowcase hanging on his doorknob. When she returned, she would find his soiled towels and linen lying in a neat pile beside his door.

Impelled by curiosity, Mrs. Buhler once entered the room with her master key. There was not so much as a hair to mar the bare tidiness. A comb and brush on the dresser, and a pile of newspapers were the only visible evidences of occupancy. The oil stove was gathering dust in the corner; it had never been used. She carried it out with her; it would be just the thing for that old lady in the north room who always complained of the cold in the afternoons, when the rest of the hotel was not uncomfortable enough to justify turning on the steam.

The old lady was sitting in the lobby one afternoon when he came home from work.

"Is that your basement roomer?" she asked.

She watched him until he disappeared at the end of the hall.

"Oh, I couldn't think where I'd seen him. But I remember now—he's a sort of porter and general helper at that large bakery on the lower Market Street."

"I really didn't know where he worked," admitted Mrs. Buhler. "I had thought of asking him several times, but he's an awfully hard man to carry on a conversation with."

He had been at the rooming-house four months when he received his first letter. Its envelope proclaimed it a hay-fever cure advertisement.

As he was not in the habit of leaving his key at the desk, the letter remained in his box for three days. Finally Mr. Buhler handed it to him as he was passing the desk on the way to his room.

He paused to read the inscription.

"You never receive any mail," remarked Mr. Buhler. "Haven't you any family?"

"No."

"Where is your home?"

"Catawissa, Pennsylvania."

"That's a funny name. How do you spell it?"

Scannon spelled it, and went on down the hall.

"C-a-t-a-w-i-double s-a," repeated Mr. Buhler to his wife. "Ain't that a funny name?"

In his room, Scannon removed the advertisement from its envelope and read it soberly from beginning to end.

Finished, he folded it and placed it on his pile of newspapers. Then he brushed his hair and went out again.

He ate supper at one of the little lunch counters near the Civic Center. The rest of the evening he spent in the newspaper room at the public library. He picked up eastern and western papers with impartial interest, reading the whole of each page, religiously and without a change of expression, until the closing bell sounded.

He never ascended to the reference, circulation or magazine rooms. Sometimes he would take the local papers home with him and read stretched out on his bed, not seeming to notice that his hands were blue with the penetrating chill that nightly drifts in from the ocean.

On Sundays he would put on a red-striped silk shirt and a blue serge suit and take a car to Golden Gate Park. There he would sit for hours in the sun, impassively watching the hundreds of picnic parties, the squirrels, or a piece of paper retreating before the breeze. Or perhaps he would walk west to the ocean, stopping for a few minutes at each of the animal pens, and take a car home from the Cliff House.

For two years the days came and passed on in monotonous reduplication, the casual hay-fever cure circulars supplying the only touches of novelty.

Then one afternoon as he was brushing his hair, he gasped and put his hand to his throat. A sharp nausea pitched him to the floor.

Inch by inch, he dragged himself to the little table and upset it, crashing the bowl and pitcher into a dozen pieces.

His energy was spent in the effort, and he lay inert.

Mrs. Buhler consented to accompany her friend to the spiritualist's only after repeated urging, and she repented her decision as soon as she arrived there.

The fusty parlor was a north room to which the sun never penetrated, and in consequence was cold and damp. The medium, a fat, untidy woman whose movements were murmurous with the rustle of silk and the tinkle of tawdry ornaments, sat facing her with one hand pressed to her forehead, and delivered mysteriously-acquired information about relatives and friends.

"Who is Dave?" she asked finally.

Mrs. Buhler hastily recalled all of her husband's and her own living relatives.

"I don't know any Dave," she said.

"Yes, yes, you know him," insisted the medium. "He's in the spirit land now. There's death right at your very door!"

She put her hand to her throat and coughed in gruesome simulation of internal strangulation.

"But I don't know any Dave," reiterated Mrs. Buhler.

She regained the street with a feeling of vast relief.

"I'll never go to one of those places again!" she asserted, as she said goodbye to her friend. "It's too creepy!"

A great fog bank was rolling in majestically from the west, blotting out the sun and dripping a fine drizzle on the pavements. Drawing her coat collar closer about her neck, Mrs. Buhler plunged into the enveloping dampness and started to climb the long hill that led to her rooming-house.

Her husband's distended eyes and pale face warned her of bad news.

"Dave Scannon's dead!" he whispered hoarsely.

Dave Scannon! So that was "Dave!"

"He's been dead for two or three days," continued Mr. Buhler. "I was beating a rug in the back yard a while ago when I noticed a swarm of big blue flies buzzing about his window. It flashed over me right away that I hadn't seen him for several days. I couldn't unlock his door, because his key was on the inside, so I called the coroner and a policeman, and we broke it in. He was lying between the bed and the dresser, and the bowl and pitcher lay broken on the floor, where he had knocked it over when he fell. They're taking him out now."

Mrs. Buhler hurried to the back stairway and descended to the lower hall. Two men were carrying a long wicker basket up the little flight of steps between the back entrance and the yard. She remained straining over the banister until the basket had disappeared.

The coroner had found nothing in his room but clothing, about five dollars in change, and a faded picture in a tarnished silver frame of an anemic looking woman who might have been a mother, wife or sister.

Mrs. Buhler answered his questions nervously. Yes, the dead man had been with them about two years. They knew little of him, for he was very peculiar and never talked, and wouldn't even allow the maid to come in and clean up his room. He had said, though, that he had no family and that his home was in Catawissa, Pennsylvania. She remembered the town because it had such an odd name.

The coroner wrote to authorities in Catawissa, who replied that they could find no traces of anyone by the name of Scannon. No more mail ever came for the man except the occasional hay-fever cure circulars.

The manager of the bakery telephoned to ask if the death notice in the paper referred to the same Dave Scannon who had been working for him. He knew nothing of the man except that he had been very punctual in his duties until that final day when he did not appear.

Several weeks later, little Mrs. Varnes, who occupied a room at the rear of the second floor, stopped at the desk to leave her key. She hovered there for a few minutes of indecision, then impulsively leaned forward.

"Mrs. Buhler, I just want to ask you something," she said, lowering her voice. "One afternoon several weeks ago I saw some men carrying a long basket out of the back door, and I've been wondering what it was."

"Probably laundry," hazarded Mrs. Buhler.

"No, it was one of those baskets such as the undertakers use to carry the dead in. I've often thought about it, but I couldn't figure out who could have died in this house, so I decided I would ask you. I told my husband about it, and he said I was dreaming."

"You must have been," said Mrs. Buhler.

APRIL 1923

Copies of the first issue of *Weird Tales* are rare, but collectors claim the next one is even harder to find. Identical in size to its predecessor, the second number features a cover by R. M. Mally that illustrates Laurie McClintock & Culpeper Chunn's "The Whispering Thing," a two-part serial beginning in this issue, which also included eighteen other stories, as well as the closing portion of Otis Adelbert Kline's "The Thing of a Thousand Shapes" and an article on the occult.

The first issue had its share of inferior stories, but Volume I, Number 2 is considerably worse. Purple prose and wooden melodrama abound, as do ludicrously hyperbolic "horror," predictable plotlines and, in the case of Carroll F. Michener's "Six Feet of Willow Green," offensive ethnic stereotyping. (Incredibly, this turgid item was resurrected in the January 1953 issue).

From the handful of good pieces, I have selected J. Paul Suter's haunted house-with-a-twist tale, "Beyond the Door." Twice reprinted (in the September 1930 and May 1954 issues), it is one of the few early *Weird Tales* stories that H. P. Lovecraft deemed worthwhile.

Beyond the Door

J. PAUL SUTER

"You haven't told me yet how it happened," I said to Mrs. Malkin.

She set her lips and eyed me, sharply.

"Didn't you talk with the coroner, sir?"

"Yes, of course," I admitted, "but as I understand you found my uncle, I thought —"

"Well, I wouldn't care to say anything about it," she interrupted, with decision.

This housekeeper of my uncle's was somewhat taller than I, and much heavier—two physical preponderances which afford any woman possessing them an advantage over the inferior male. She appeared a subject for diplomacy rather than argument.

Noting her ample jaw, her breadth of cheek, the unsentimental glint of her eye, I decided on conciliation. I placed a chair for her, there in my Uncle Godfrey's study, and dropped into another, myself.

"At least, before we go over the other parts of the house, suppose we rest a little," I suggested in my most unctuous manner. "The place rather gets on one's nerves—don't you think so?"

It was sheer luck—I claim no credit for it. My chance reflection found the weak spot in her fortifications. She replied to it with an undoubted smack of satisfaction:

"It's more than seven years that I've been doing for Mr. Sarston, sir. Bringing him his meals regular as clockwork, keeping the house clean—as clean as he'd let me—and sleeping at my own home, o' nights; and in all that time I've said, over and over, there ain't a house in New York the equal of this for queerness."

"Nor anywhere else," I encouraged her, with a laugh; and her confidences opened another notch:

"You're likely right in that, too, sir. As I've said to poor Mr. Sarston, many a time, 'It's all well enough,' says I, 'to have bugs for a hobby. You can afford it; and being a bachelor and by yourself, you don't have to consider other people's likes and dislikes. And it's all well enough if you want to,' says I, 'to keep thousands and thousands o' them in cabinets all over the place, the way you do. But when it comes to pinnin' them on the walls in regular armies,' I says, 'and on the ceiling of your own study, and even on different parts of furniture, so that a body don't know what awful things she's agoin' to find under her hand of a sudden when she does the dusting; why then,' I says to him, 'it's drivin' a decent woman too far.' "

"And did he never try to reform his ways when you told him that?" I asked, smiling.

"To be frank with you, Mr. Robinson, when I talked like that to him, he generally raised my pay. And what was a body to do then?"

"I can't see how Lucy Lawton stood the place as long as she did," I observed, watching Mrs. Malkin's red face very closely.

She swallowed the bait and leaned forward, hands on knees.

"Poor girl, it got on her nerves. But she was the quiet kind. You never saw her, sir?"

I shook my head.

"One of them slim, faded girls with light hair, and hardly a word to say for herself. I don't believe she got to know the next-door neighbor in the whole year she lived with your uncle. She was an orphan, wasn't she, sir?"

"Yes," I said. "Godfrey Sarston and I were her only living relatives. That was why she came from Australia to stay with him, after her father's death."

Mrs. Malkin nodded. I was hoping that, putting a check on my eagerness, I could lead her on to a number of things I greatly desired to know. Up to the time I had induced the housekeeper to show me through this strange house of my Uncle Godfrey's, the whole affair had been a mystery of lips which closed and faces which were averted at my approach. Even the coroner seemed unwilling to tell me just how my uncle had died.

"Did you understand she was going to live with him, sir?" asked Mrs. Malkin, looking hard at me.

I confined myself to a nod.

"Well, so did I. Yet after a year, back she went."

"She went suddenly?" I suggested.

"So suddenly that I never knew a thing about it till after she was gone. I came to do my chores one day, and she was here. I came the next, and she had started back to Australia. That's how sudden she went."

"They must have had a falling out," I conjectured. "I suppose it was because of the house."

"Maybe it was and maybe it wasn't."

"You know of other reasons?"

"I have eyes in my head," she said. "But I'm not going to talk about it. Shall we be getting on now, sir?"

I tried another lead: "I hadn't seen my uncle in five years, you know. He seemed terribly changed. He was not an old man, by any means, yet when I saw him at the funeral —" I paused, expectantly.

To my relief, she responded readily: "He looked that way for the last few months, especially that last week. I spoke to him about it, two days before—before it happened, sir—and told him he'd do well to see the doctor again. But he cut me off short. My sister took sick the same day, and I was called out of town. The next time I saw him, he was —"

She paused, and then went on, sobbing: "To think of him lyin' there in that awful place, and callin' and callin' for me, as I know he must and me not around to hear him!"

As she stopped again, suddenly, and threw a suspicious glance at me, I hastened to insert a matter-of-fact question: "Did he appear ill on that last day?"

"Not so much ill, as —"

"Yes?" I prompted.

She was silent a long time, while I waited, afraid that some word of mine had brought back her former attitude of hostility.

Then she seemed to make up her mind. "I oughtn't to say another word. I've said too much, already. But you've been liberal with me, sir, and I know somethin' you've a right to be told, which I'm thinkin' no one else is agoin' to tell you. Look at the bottom of his study door a minute, sir."

I followed her direction. What I saw led me to drop to my hands and knees the better to examine it.

"Why should he put a rubber strip on the bottom of his door?" I asked, getting up.

She replied with another enigmatical suggestion: "Look at these, if you will, sir. You'll remember that he slept in this study. That was his bed, over there in the alcove."

"Bolts!" I exclaimed. And I reinforced sight with touch by shooting one of them back and forth a few times. "Double bolts on the inside of his bedroom door! An upstairs room, at that. What was the idea?"

Mrs. Malkin portentously shook her head and sighed, as one unburdening her mind. "Only this can I say, sir; he was afraid of something—terribly afraid, sir. Something that came in the night."

"What was it?" I demanded.

"I don't know, sir."

"It was in the night that—it happened?" I asked.

She nodded; then, as if the prologue were over, as if she had prepared my mind sufficiently, she produced something from under her apron. She must have been holding it there all the time.

"It's his diary, sir. It was lying here on the floor. I saved it for you, before the police could get their hands on it."

I opened the little book. One of the sheets near the back was crumpled, and I glanced at it, idly.

What I read there impelled me to slap the cover shut again.

"Did you read this?" I demanded.

She met my gaze, frankly.

"I looked into it, sir, just as you did—only just looked into it. Not for worlds would I do even that again!"

"I noticed some reference here to a slab in the cellar. What slab is that?"

"It covers an old, dried-up well, sir."

"Will you show it to me?"

"You can find it for yourself, sir, if you wish. I'm not goin' down there," she said, decidedly.

"Ah, well, I've seen enough for today," I told her. "I'll take the diary back to my hotel and read it."

I did not return to my hotel, however. In my one brief glance into the little book, I had seen something which had bitten into my soul, only a few words, but they had brought me very near to that queer, solitary man who had been my uncle.

I dismissed Mrs. Malkin and remained in the study. There was the fitting place to read the diary he had left behind him. His personality lingered like a vapor in that study. I settled into his deep morris chair and turned it to catch the light from the single, narrow window—the light, doubtless, by which he had written much of his work on entomology.

That same struggling illumination played shadowy tricks with hosts of wall-crucified insects, which seemed engaged in a united effort to crawl upward in sinuous lines. Some of their number, impaled to the ceiling itself, peered quiveringly down on the aspiring multitude. The whole house, with its crisp dead, rustling in any vagrant breeze, brought back to my mind the hand that had pinned them, one by one, on wall and ceiling and furniture. A kindly hand, I reflected, though eccentric; one not to be turned aside from its single hobby.

When quiet, peering Uncle Godfrey went, there passed out another of those scientific enthusiasts whose passion for exact truth in some one direction has extended the bounds of human knowledge. Could not his unquestioned merits have been balanced against his sin? Was it necessary to even-handed justice that he die face-to-face with the thing he most feared? I ponder the question still, though his body—strangely bruised—has been long at rest.

The entries in the little book began with the fifteenth of June. Everything before that date had been torn out. There, in the room where it had been written, I read my Uncle Godfrey's diary.

"It is done. I am trembling so that the words will hardly form under my pen, but my mind is collected. My course was for the best. Suppose I had married her? She would have been unwilling to live in this house. At the outset, her wishes would have come between me and my work, and that would have been only the beginning.

"As a married man, I could not have concentrated properly. I could not have surrounded myself with the atmosphere indispensable to the writing of my book. My scientific message would never have been delivered. As it is, though my heart is sore, I shall stifle these memories in work.

"I wish I had been more gentle with her, especially when she sank to her knees before me, tonight. She kissed my hand. I should not have repulsed her so roughly. In particular, my words could have been better chosen. I said to her, bitterly: 'Get up, and don't nuzzle my hand like a dog.' She rose, without a word, and left me. How was I to know that, within an hour —

"I am largely to blame. Yet, had I taken any other course afterward than the one I did, the authorities would have misunderstood."

Again, there followed a space from which the sheets had been torn; but from the sixteenth of July, all the pages were intact. Something had come over the writing, too. It was still precise and clear—my Uncle Godfrey's characteristic hand—but the letters were less firm. As the entries approached the end, this difference became still more marked.

Here follows, then, the whole of his story; or as much of it as will ever be known. I shall let his words speak for him, without further interruption:

"My nerves are becoming more seriously affected. If certain annoyances do not shortly cease, I shall be obliged to procure medical advice. To be more specific, I find myself, at times, obsessed by an almost uncontrollable desire to descend to the cellar and lift the slab over the old well.

"I never have yielded to the impulse, but it has persisted for minutes together with such intensity that I have had to put work aside and literally hold myself down in my chair. This insane desire comes only in the dead of night, when its disquieting effect is heightened by the various noises peculiar to the house.

"For instance, there often is a draft of air along the hallways, which causes a rustling among the specimens impaled on the walls. Lately, too, there have been other nocturnal sounds, strongly suggestive of the busy clamor of rats and mice. This calls for investigation. I have been at considerable expense to make the house proof against rodents, which might destroy some of my best specimens. If some structural defect has opened a way for them, the situation must be corrected at once.

"July 17th. The foundations and cellar were examined today by a workman. He states positively that there is no place of ingress for rodents. He contented himself with looking at the slab over the old well, without lifting it.

"July 19th. While I was sitting in this chair, late last night, writing, the impulse to descend to the cellar suddenly came upon me with tremendous insistence. I yielded—which, perhaps, was as well. For at least I satisfied myself that the disquiet which possesses me has no external cause.

"The long journey through the hallways was difficult. Several times, I was keenly aware of the same sounds (perhaps I should say, the same IMPRESSIONS of sounds) that I had erroneously laid to rats. I am convinced now that they are more symptoms of my nervous condition. Further indications of this came in the fact that, as I opened the cellar door, the small noises abruptly ceased. There was no final scamper of tiny footfalls to suggest rats disturbed at their occupations.

"Indeed, I was conscious of a certain impression of expectant silence—as if the thing behind the noises, whatever it was, had paused to watch me enter its domain. Throughout my time in the cellar, I seemed surrounded by this same atmosphere. Sheer 'nerves,' of course.

"In the main, I held myself well under control. As I was about to leave the cellar, however, I unguardedly glanced back over my shoulder at the stone slab covering the old well. At that, a violent tremor came over me, and, losing all command, I rushed back up the cellar stairs, thence to this study. My nerves are playing me sorry tricks.

"July 30th. For more than a week, all has been well. The tone of my nerves seems distinctly better. Mrs. Malkin, who has remarked several times lately upon my paleness, expressed the conviction this afternoon that I am nearly my old self again. This is encouraging. I was beginning to fear that the severe strain of the past few months had left an indelible mark upon me. With continued health, I shall be able to finish my book by spring.

"July 31st. Mrs. Malkin remained rather late tonight in connection with some item of housework, and it was quite dark when I returned to my study from bolting the street door after her. The blackness of the upper hall, which the former owner of the house inexplicably failed to wire for electricity, was profound. As I came to the top of the second flight of stairs, something clutched at my foot, and, for an instant, almost pulled me back. I freed myself and ran to the study.

"August 3rd. Again the awful insistence. I sit here, with this diary upon my knees, and it seems that fingers of iron are tearing at me. I WILL NOT go! My nerves may be utterly unstrung again (I fear they are), but I am still their master.

"August 4th. I did not yield, last night. After a bitter struggle, which must have lasted nearly an hour, the desire to go to the cellar suddenly departed. I must not give in at any time.

"August 5th. Tonight, the rat noises (I shall call them that for want of a more appropriate term) are very noticeable. I went to the length of unbolting my door and stepping into the hallway to listen. After a few minutes, I seemed to be aware of something large and grey watching me from the darkness at the end of the passage. This is a bizarre statement, of course, but it exactly describes my impression. I withdrew hastily into the study, and bolted the door.

"Now that my nerves' condition is so palpably affecting the optic nerve, I must not much longer delay seeing a specialist. But—how much shall I tell him?

"August 8th. Several times tonight, while sitting here at my work, I have seemed to hear soft footsteps in the passage. 'Nerves,' again, of course, or else some new trick of the wind among the specimens on the walls.

"August 9th. By my watch it is four o'clock in the morning. My mind is made up to record the experience I have passed through. Calmness may come that way.

"Feeling rather fatigued last night, from the strain of a weary day of research, I retired early. My sleep was more refreshing than usual, as it is likely to be when one is genuinely tired. I awakened, however (it must have been about an hour ago), with a start of tremendous violence.

"There was moonlight in the room. My nerves were on edge, but for a moment, I saw nothing unusual. Then, glancing toward the door, I perceived what appeared to be thin, white fingers thrust under it—exactly as if someone outside the door were trying to attract my attention in that manner. I rose and turned on the light, but the fingers were gone.

"Needless to say, I did not open the door. I write the occurrence down, just as it took place, or as it seemed; but I cannot trust myself to comment upon it.

"August 10th. Have fastened heavy rubber strips on the bottom of my bedroom door.

"August 15th. All quiet, for several nights. I am hoping that the rubber strips, being something definite and tangible, have had a salutary effect upon my nerves. Perhaps I shall not need to see a doctor.

"August 17th. Once more, I have been aroused from sleep. The interruptions seem to come always at the same hour—about three o'clock in the morning. I had been dreaming of the well in the cellar—the same dream, over and over—everything black except the slab, and a figure with bowed head and averted face seated there. Also, I had vague dreams about a dog. Can it be that my last words to her have impressed that on my mind? I must pull myself together. In particular, I must not, under any pressure, yield, and visit the cellar after nightfall.

"August 18th. Am feeling much more hopeful. Mrs. Malkin remarked on it, while serving dinner. This improvement is due largely to a consultation I have had with Dr. Sartwell, the distinguished specialist in nervous diseases. I went into full details with him, excepting certain reservations. He scouted the idea that my experiences could be other than purely mental.

"When he recommended a change of scene (which I had been expecting), I told him positively that it was out of the question. He said then that, with the aid of a tonic and an occasional sleeping draft, I am likely to progress well enough at home. This is distinctly encouraging. I erred in not going to him at the start. Without doubt, most, if not all, of my hallucinations could have been averted.

"I have been suffering a needless penalty from my nerves for an action I took solely in the interests of science. I have no disposition to tolerate it further. From today, I shall report regularly to Dr. Sartwell.

"August 19th. Used the sleeping draft last night, with gratifying results. The doctor says I must repeat the dose for several nights, until my nerves are well under control again.

"August 21st. All well. It seems that I have found the way out—a very simple and prosaic way. I might have avoided much needless annoyance by seeking expert advice at the beginning. Before retiring last night, I unbolted my study door and took a turn up and down the passage. I felt no trepidation. The place was as it used to be, before these fancies assailed me. A visit to the cellar after nightfall will be the test for my complete recovery, but I am not quite ready for that. Patience!

"August 22nd. I have just read yesterday's entry, thinking to steady myself. It is cheerful—almost gay; and there are other entries like it in preceding pages. I am a mouse in the grip of a cat. Let me have freedom for ever so short a time, and I begin to rejoice at my escape. Then the paw descends again.

"It is four in the morning—the usual hour. I retired rather late last night, after administering the draft. Instead of the dreamless sleep, which heretofore has followed the use of the drug, the slumber into which I fell was punctuated by recurrent visions of the slab, with the bowed figure upon it. Also, I had one poignant dream in which the dog was involved.

"At length, I awakened and reached mechanically for the light switch beside my bed. When my hand encountered nothing, I suddenly realized the truth. I was standing in my study, with my other hand upon the doorknob. It required only a moment, of course, to find the light and switch it on. I saw then that the bolt had been drawn back. The door was quite unlocked. My awakening must have interrupted me in the very act of opening it. I could hear something moving restlessly in the passage outside the door.

"August 23rd. I must beware of sleeping at night. Without confiding the fact to Dr. Sartwell, I have begun to take the drug in the daytime. At first, Mrs. Malkin's views were pronounced, but my explanation of 'doctor's orders' has silenced her. I am awake for breakfast and supper, and sleep in the hours between. She is leaving me, each evening, a cold lunch to be eaten at midnight.

"August 26th. Several times, I have caught myself nodding in my chair. The last time, I am sure that, on arousing, I perceived the rubber strip under the door bent inward, as if something were pushing it from the other side. I must not, under any circumstances, permit myself to fall asleep.

"September 2nd. Mrs. Malkin is to be away, because of her sister's illness. I cannot help dreading her absence. Though she is here only in the daytime, even that companionship is very welcome.

"September 3rd. Let me put this into writing. The mere labor of composition has a soothing influence upon me. God knows, I need such an influence now, as never before!

"In spite of all my watchfulness, I fell asleep tonight—across my bed. I must have been utterly exhausted. The dream I had was the one about the dog. I was patting the creature's head, over and over.

"I awoke, at last, to find myself in darkness, and in a standing position. There was a suggestion of chill and earthiness in the air. While I was drowsily trying to get my bearings, I became aware that something was muzzling my hand, as a dog might do.

"Still saturated with my dream, I was not greatly astonished. I extended my hand to pat the dog's head. That brought me to my senses. I was standing in the cellar.

"THE THING BEFORE ME WAS NOT A DOG!

"I cannot tell how I fled back up the cellar stairs. I know, however, that as I turned, the slab was visible, in spite of the darkness, with something sitting upon it. All the way up the stairs, hands snatched at my feet . . ."

*   *   *

This entry seemed to finish this diary, for blank pages followed it; but I remembered the crumpled sheet, near the back of the book. It was partly torn out, as if a hand had clutched it, convulsively. The writing on it, too, was markedly in contrast to the precise, albeit nervous penmanship of even the last entry I had perused. I was forced to hold the scrawl up to the light to decipher it. This is what I read: "My hand keeps on writing, in spite of myself. What is this? I do not wish to write, but it compels me. Yes, yes, I will tell the truth, I will tell the truth."

A heavy blot followed, partly covering the writing. With difficulty, I made it out:

"The guilt is mine—mine, only. I loved her too well, yet I was unwilling to marry, though she entreated me on her knees—though she kissed my hand. I told her my scientific work came first. She did it, herself. I was not expecting that—I swear I was not expecting it. But I was afraid the authorities would misunderstand. So I took what seemed the best course. She had no friends here who would inquire.

"It is waiting outside my door. I *feel* it. It compels me, through my thoughts. My hand keeps on writing. I must not fall asleep. I must think only of what I am writing. I must —"

Then came the words I had seen when Mrs. Malkin had handed me the book. They were written very large. In places, the pen had dug through the paper. Though they were scrawled, I read them at a glance:

"Not the slab in the cellar! Not that! Oh, my God, anything but that! Anything —"

By what strange compulsion was the hand forced to write down what was in the brain; even to the ultimate thoughts; even to those final words?

The grey light from outside, slanting down through two dull little windows, sank into the sodden hole near the inner wall. The coroner and I stood in the cellar, but not too near the hole.

A small, demonstrative, dark man—the chief of detectives—stood a little apart from us, his eyes intent, his natural animation suppressed. We were watching the stooped shoulders of a police constable, who was angling in the well.

"See anything, Walters?" inquired the detective, raspingly.

The policeman shook his head.

The little man turned his questioning to me.

"You're quite sure?" he demanded.

"Ask the coroner. He saw the diary," I told him.

"I'm afraid there can be no doubt," the coroner confirmed in his heavy, tired voice.

He was an old man, with lackluster eyes. It had seemed best to me, on the whole, that he should read my uncle's diary. His position entitled him to all the available facts. What we were seeking in the well might especially concern him.

He looked at me opaquely now, while the policeman bent double again. Then he spoke—like one who reluctantly and at last does his duty. He nodded toward the slab of grey stone, which lay in the shadow to the left of the well.

"It doesn't seem very heavy, does it?" he suggested, in an undertone.

I shook my head. "Still, it's stone," I demurred. "A man would have to be rather strong to lift it."

"To lift it—yes." He glanced about the cellar. "Ah, I forgot," he said, abruptly. "It is in my office, as part of the evidence." He went on, half to himself: "A man—even though not very strong—could take a stick—for instance, the stick that is now in my office—and prop up the slab. If he wished to look into the well," he whispered.

The policeman interrupted, straightening again with a groan, and laying his electric torch beside the well. "It's breaking my back," he complained. "There's dirt down there. It seems loose, but I can't get through it. Somebody'll have to go down."

The detective cut it: "I'm lighter than you, Walters."

"I'm not afraid, sir."

"I didn't say you were," the little man snapped. "There's nothing down there, anyway—though we'll have to prove that, I suppose." He glanced truculently at me, but went on talking to the constable: "Rig the rope around me, and don't bungle the knot. I've no intention of falling into the place."

"There is something there," whispered the coroner, slowly, to me. His eyes left the little detective and the policeman, carefully tying and testing knots, and turned again to the square slab of stone. "Suppose—while a man was looking into that hole—with the stone propped up—he should accidentally knock the prop away?" He was still whispering.

"A stone so light that he could prop it up wouldn't be heavy enough to kill him," I objected.

"No." He laid a hand on my shoulder. "Not to kill him—to paralyze him—if it struck the spine in a certain way. To render him helpless, but not unconscious. The post mortem would disclose that, through the bruises on the body."

The policeman and the detective had adjusted the knots to their satisfaction. They were bickering now as to the details of the descent.

"Would that cause death?" I whispered.

"You must remember that the housekeeper was absent for two days. In two days, even that pressure —" He stared at me hard, to make sure that I understood—"with the head down —"

Again the policeman interrupted: "I'll stand at the well, if you gentlemen will grab the rope behind me. It won't be much of a pull. I'll take the brunt of it."

We let the little man down, with the electric torch strapped to his waist, and some sort of implement—a trowel or a small spade—in his hand. It seemed a long time before his voice, curiously hollow, directed us to stop. The hole must have been deep. We braced ourselves. I was second, the coroner, last. The policeman relieved his strain somewhat by snagging the rope against the edge of the well.

A noise like muffled scratching reached us from below. Occasionally, the rope shook and shifted slightly at the edge of the hole. At last, the detective's hollow voice spoke.

"What does he say?" the coroner demanded.

The policeman turned his square, dogged face toward us.

"I think he's found something," he explained.

The rope jerked and shifted again. Some sort of struggle seemed to be going on below. The weight suddenly increased, and as suddenly lessened, as if something had been grasped, then had managed to elude the grasp and slip away. I could catch the detective's rapid breathing now; also the sound of inarticulate speech in his hollow voice.

The next words I caught more clearly. They were a command to pull him up. At the same moment, the weight on the rope grew heavier, and remained so.

The policeman's big shoulders began straining, rhythmically.

"All together," he directed. "Take it easy. Pull when I do."

Slowly, the rope passed through our hands. Then it tightened suddenly, and there was an ejaculation from below—just below. Still holding fast, the policeman contrived to stoop over and look. He translated the ejaculation for us. "Let down a little. He's stuck with it against the side." We slackened the rope, until the detective's voice gave us the word again.

The rhythmic tugging continued. Something dark appeared, quite abruptly, at the top of the hole. My nerves leapt inside of me, but it was merely the top of the detective's head—his dark hair. Something white came next—his pale face, with starting eyes. Then his shoulders, bowed forward, the better to support what was in his arms. Then —

I looked away; but as he laid his burden down at the side of the well, the detective whispered to us: "He had her covered up with dirt—covered up . . ."

He began to laugh—a little, high cackle, like a child's—until the coroner took him by the shoulders and deliberately shook him. Then the policeman led him out of the cellar.

It was not then, but afterward, that I put my question to the coroner.

"Tell me," I demanded. "People pass there at all hours. Why didn't my uncle call for help?"

"I have thought of that," he replied. "I believe he did call. I think, probably, he screamed. But his head was down, and he couldn't raise it. His screams must have been swallowed up in the well."

"You are sure he didn't murder her?" He had given me that assurance before, but I wished it again.

"Almost sure," he declared. "Though it was on his account, undoubtedly, that she killed herself. Few of us are punished as accurately for our sins as he was."

One should be thankful, even for crumbs of comfort. I am thankful.

But there are times when my uncle's face rises before me. After all, we were the same blood, our sympathies had much in common; under any given circumstances our thoughts and feelings must have been largely the same. I seem to see him in that final death march along the unlighted passageway—obeying an imperative summons—going on, step by step—down the stairway to the first floor, down the cellar stairs—at last, lifting the slab.

I try not to think of the final expiation. Yet was it final? I wonder. Did the last Door of all, when it opened, find him willing to pass through? Or was something waiting beyond that Door?

MAY 1923

Two changes distinguish issue #3: interior illustrations, mostly by unnamed artists, were added and size was increased from 6" x 9" to what *Weird Tales* historian Bob Weinberg calls "large bedsheet size."

The percentage of good stories is slightly higher than the second issue. The first of *Weird Tales*'s long series of reprinted stories appears, Edward Bulwer-Lytton's "The Haunters and the Haunted" (also known as "The House and the Brain"). The serials continue to be less than inspired, with the end of "The Whispering Thing" upstaged by the first half of "The Moon Terror," a contrived bit of Asian-bashing "science-fiction" that racked up the highest sales till then for any issue. Encouraged by its popularity, the publishers rushed to publish "The Moon Terror" as a book, but reader enthusiasm did not last. Copies of it cluttered up the editorial offices well into the 1940s.

Counting the serials and Bulwer-Lytton's classic, Volume I, Number 3 consists of twenty-one stories, including a clever bit of whimsy by the novelist Vincent Starrett, best remembered today as a Chicago Tribune literary columnist and as the author of the indispensable Holmesian study, "The Private Life of Sherlock Holmes" (not to be confused with the Billy Wilder film of the same name).

Another story in the third issue, M. L. Humphrey's "The Floor Above," was well-liked by H. P. Lovecraft, but I do not share his enthusiasm.

I chose Herman Sisk's offbeat haunted cabin tale, "The Purple Heart," and Lyle Wilson Holden's "The Devil Plant," which, though a bit overwritten, is worth noting as a forerunner of "Audrey II" from "Little Shop of Horrors." It is one of several "malevolent vegetable" stories to appear in the pages of "The Unique Magazine."

The Devil Plant

LYLE WILSON HOLDEN

It was the last straw! Injury upon injury I had borne without a murmur, but now I determined to revenge myself upon Silvela Castelar, let the cost be what it would. His malevolent influence has pursued me since early boyhood, and it was he who caused every fond hope of my life to turn to ashes before its realization.

Long ago, when we were boys in school together, his evil work began. We were both of Spanish blood, and both, having lost our parents in childhood, were being educated by our respective guardians at one of the famous boys' schools of England.

Nothing was more natural in the circumstances, than that we should become chums and room-mates. However, it was not long before I began to be sorry that I had entered into such close relationship with him. He was absolutely unscrupulous, and soon his escapades won him an unenviable reputation among the other students, although he always managed, by skillfully covering his trail, to stand well with the authorities of the school.

Before many weeks had passed, a particularly heinous outrage, which he had committed, set the whole school in an uproar. It could not be overlooked, and a strict investigation was started.

What was my horror to discover that his devilish ingenuity had woven a web of evidence which thoroughly enmeshed me within its coils! There was no escape: I was dismissed in disgrace from the school, and in disgrace I left England. The notoriety I received in many of the leading papers of the Kingdom made it impossible for me to enter another school or to obtain any honest employment.

I came to America, working my passage over upon a cattle ship. The years that followed were hard ones, but by sober industry I forged slowly ahead until, at last, I had bright prospects of becoming the junior partner in a large business house in Baltimore.

Then my evil genius appeared. Silvela obtained employment in our company, and by his devilish cunning soon made himself well liked and trusted.

Then one morning, a few months after he came, it was reported that a large amount of money had been stolen from the firm. Again

a network of circumstantial evidence pointed indisputably in my
direction.

I was arrested and brought to trail. The evidence not being
entirely conclusive, the jury disagreed, and I was set free; but my
career in America was forever blasted.

As soon as I could close up my affairs, I buried myself in the
wilds of Australia, where I began life anew. Fortune was kind to me
and I prospered. Under another name, I became a respected and
honored citizen of a thriving new settlement.

Then the crowning blessing of all came when I won the love of
the beautiful Mercedes, a black-eyed, olive-hued immigrant from
my old province of Andalusia. Then, indeed, I was at the threshold
of Heaven! But how short was my day of bliss!

Four weeks before our wedding day Silvela Castelar suddenly
entered our settlement. It is useless to dwell upon that wretched
period. Sufficient to say that this hellborn fiend again worked his
diabolic sorcery, and Mercedes was lost to me forever.

The report came to me that Silvela, for the first time in his life,
loved with a fierce, consuming passion, and that Mercedes soon
would be betrothed to him. Then it was that I vowed by all that was
holy that Silvela Castelar should pay in full his guilty debt, even
though, as a result, my soul should sink into stygian blackness.

Why do I write this? Because I take a grim pleasure in telling of
my revenge, and because I want the world to know that I had just
provocation. I am not afraid. Life or death—it matters little which
is my portion now. When this is read I shall be far from the haunts
of men.

Silvela Castelar thought I was a fool. It suited my purpose that
he should continue to think so. I treated him as a bosom friend, and
he, poor idiot, thought I never guessed that he was the instigator of
the ruin which drove me from England, wrecked my business career
in America, and in the end left me desolate, without hope of ever
enjoying the blessings of love.

So, while we smoked, read, or hunted together, I brooded upon
my wrongs, and racked my brain for some method by which I could
accomplish that which was now the sole absorbing motive of my
life. Then chance threw across my path the instrument of my
vengeance.

One day, while I was wandering, desolate and alone, through a wild and unexplored part of the country, I came upon one of the rarest and at the same time one of the most terrible species of the vegetable kingdom ever discovered. It is know as the octopus plant, called by the natives "the devil tree." When I saw it my heart gave a throb of exultation, for I knew that my search was ended; the means by which I could accomplish my purpose was now at had.

Silvela and I had but one passion in common—an intense love for botanical investigation. I knew that he would be interested when he heard of my strange discovery, and I believed that his knowledge of the plant was not sufficient to make him cautious. On the evening of the next day but one, as we sat smoking, I broached the subject.

"Silvela, in the old days you used to be considerably wrapped up in the study of plant life. Are you still interested?"

"Somewhat," he replied, and then his eyes narrowed craftily. "I exhausted the interesting possibilities of most of the known plants of the world a number of years ago. Lately I have found 'the light that lies in women's eyes' a subject of greater interest."

I could have strangled him where he sat; but a lifetime of trouble has taught me to conceal my feelings. I betrayed no emotion.

"I'll venture that there is one plant which you have never studied at first hand."

"What is that?" he asked, with mild curiosity.

"A plant," I continued, "found only in the most inaccessible places of the earth. Probably it could be seen only in the wildest parts of Sumatra or Australia, and then scarcely once in a lifetime."

He was now thoroughly aroused.

"What is the family of this wonderful shrub?" he asked. "I have a dim recollection of having heard of it. Let me see—isn't it called —"

"The devil tree by the natives, by others the octopus plant," I broke in. "But I have heard that the name is somewhat of a misnomer. It is said that it is rather a tree of heaven, for it distills a rare and delicious nectar which has a wonderful rejuvenating power. At the same time in intoxicates in a strange and mysterious manner, causing him who drinks to revel in celestial visions of love and radiant beauty. Instead of leaving one depressed, as is the case with alcohol, it is said that the impression lingers, the face grows younger, and he who sips is actually loved by any of the female sex whose eyes look upon him. Indeed, I have heard that if our countryman, Ponce de

Leon, had gone to the South Seas instead of to Florida, he would have really discovered the fountain of youth for which he sought."

I looked at Silvela. His eyes were sparkling, and he was breathing quickly: I knew I had found his weak point. His was a dreamy, half-superstitious nature, and my words appealed to him strongly.

"Ah!" he exclaimed. "Would that I could see this marvelous phenomenon and sip of its celestial juice!"

"It could be done," I replied, hesitatingly, "but it would involve some hardship and considerable danger."

"Did you ever see one of these plants?"

"Yes; not two days since."

Silvela sprang to his feet, with a Spanish oath.

"*Dios mio!*" he cried. "Rodriguez, why did you not tell me? When can we start to find it?"

"Softly," I admonished. "I told you there was danger. Haven't you heard that this devil's plant has been known to forge itself upon human flesh?"

"The wild story of some frightened native," he scoffed. "Take me to it and nothing shall prevent me from testing the fabled powers of its juices. Stop! Did you not drink of this delicious nectar?"

I shook my head sadly.

"No, I had no wish to try. Why should I seek to become young in body when my heart is old within?"

"You were afraid," he sneered, "afraid of the trailing tendrils of this plant devil."

"Have it that way if you wish," I answered indifferently. "However, if in spite of my warning, you still persist in wishing to see this strange freak of nature, I will do my best to guide you to it; but I repeat, the way is long and difficult, and you had better leave this cursed thing alone."

"We will start in the morning," he asserted decisively, as he arose to leave.

I said nothing more, but, alone in my room, I laughed like a devil at the success of my ruse.

Next morning the weather was squally and tempestuous, and I was afraid that the fire of Silvela's enthusiasm would be burning low. But I also knew that opposition would be fuel to the flame.

"I fear we shall have to postpone our journey," I remarked, when he appeared.

If Silvela had any doubts as to the advisability of our starting out that morning, they vanished at once.

"Nonsense!" he rasped. "It is fine weather for our purpose."

"All right, my friend," I replied. "Remember, though, that I advised against going."

"The consequences be upon my head," he rejoined. "Come, let us be on our way."

Our path was strewn with difficulties, and we progressed but slowly. At times the wind howled and whistled across the wild spaces with a sound so mournful that it sent a shudder through me. The heavens were murky, and low, dark clouds raced across the leaden sky as though fleeing form some scene of horror. Great rocks impeded our progress at every step, and their grotesque forms seemed to leer at us evilly as we passed. At length Silvela paused and mopped his brow.

"Come," I exclaimed, "you are tired and exhauted. The day is declining. Let us go back."

Silvela hesitated, and there was an instant in which I was afraid he would take me at my word. Then he straightened, and his chin set determinedly.

"No. We have come far; we will continue to the end."

I thought a tremor passed over Silvela's sturdy form and that his face paled slightly, but he turned resolutely and followed me as I pushed forward once more.

It was late in the afternoon when we approached the end of our journey. The clouds had become less dense, and the sun, hanging upon the horizon, gleamed through with a sullen glare. The whole western sky bore the appearance of curdled blood.

At length I led the way around an immense rock, stopped, and pointed to the north. There, but a short distance ahead, stood the ghastly plant.

It was, in appearance, like a huge pineapple about ten or twelve feet in height. From the top sprang the broad, dark green leaves, trailing downward to the ground and enclosing the plant in a kind of cage.

Inside these leaves, at the top of its bulky body, could be seen two round, fleshy plates, one above the other. Dripping constantly from these was a golden, intoxicating nectar, the fatal lure that tempts the victim to his fate. Surrounding these plates were long green tendrils or arms like those upon an octopus. A slight pressure upon one of these disks would cause the serpent-like tendrils to enfold the victim in their deadly embrace, while the sweet fluid rendered the poor wretch oblivious to danger until it was too late.

Silvela stood for a moment silently looking at the strange plant at which I pointed.

"It is an uncanny sight," he muttered, and a shiver ran over his body.

"Uncanny it is, indeed," I replied. "I, for one, have no desire to make a closer acquaintance."

"You were always ready to show the white feather," he derided scornfully.

I did not openly resent this; I could bear insult for a little while longer.

"Silvela," I said, "Let us leave this dreadful plant alone. I implore you to return with me now. You have seen this horrid thing, why should you care to test the legendary power of the fluid which it distills?"

"Because I love," he replied in a dreamy voice, "and I wish to be loved beyond all men. If it be, indeed, the fountain of youth, what danger can deter me from sipping its miraculous juice?"

"Then I will say no more. Drink, then, of the fabled wonders of this tree of destiny, and may all the joy and all the happiness to which your life entitles you, come to you as you drink the nectar that drips in golden drops from its heart."

Silvela darted a quick look at me from his dark eyes, as though half suspecting a hidden meaning in my words. Then he stepped quickly toward the ominous plant.

"Careful!" I cautioned, "Do not touch the long, green tendrils. There is where the danger lies, for they might tear your flesh."

Silvela stood for an instant close beside the trailing arms, his eyes glowing with a half insane light. His face was flushed with the passionate fire that surged through his veins. To his susceptible mind I know that it was the crowning adventure of his life. I could tell that his heart was pounding, from the throbbing arteries of his throat. His lips were moving, and I strained my ears to catch the sound.

"For Mercedes!" he murmured, and stepped between the hanging tendrils.

Another moment's pause, and he bent down to the fleshy plates in the heart of the plant and drank long and deeply of the golden juice. Dreamily he closed his eyes, and, leaning forward, I could faintly catch some of the broken accents that came from his lips.

"Ah, love, my only love!" he murmured, "See, beloved, the angel faces—celestial voices coming near—sweet, how sweet—unearthly light of elysian fields—ah, the heavenly perfume—the surging of the eternal sea!"

With folded arms, I stood and waited. Lost to all else save the delights of his entrancing vision, every faculty, every sense deluded into happy quiescence by the chimerical phantasm, he did not note the tremulous vibrations which ran through the whole mass of the horrible plant.

Slowly at first, and then more quickly, the long, sinewy palpi began to rise and twist in what seemed a fearful dance of death. Higher and higher rose the dreadful arms, until they hovered over the unconscious form of their victim.

Once I pressed a little too closely, and one of the awful, twisting tendrils came in contact with my hand. I sprang back and just in time for so deadly was the grasp of the noxious arms, that the skin was stripped from my flesh.

Slowly, but surely, the octopuslike arms settled about Silvela's body. One of them dropped across his cheek. As it touched the bare flesh a tremor ram through his frame, and he suddenly opened his eyes.

It was only a moment until he was fully awake to the horror of his position. While he was reveling in dreams of paradise, the grim arms of the death plant had enclosed him in their viselike clasp, and I knew that no power upon earth could make them relax until they opened to throw forth the dry husk—the dead skin and bones—of their prey. Already they had so constricted his chest that he could breathe only in short, panting gasps. His terror-stricken eyes sought my face.

"My God, Rodriguez!" he cried in a terrible voice.

The arms gripped him closer. He gasped out a word, *"Help!"*

"Silvela Castelar," I said, with quiet bitterness, "You are beyond all human aid. I could not help you if I would. Once within the grasp of those awful arms, I would be as helpless as you. Remember at every step of this fatal journey I warned you, but at each warning you grew more determined. Three times you have brought ruin upon me; the third time you left for me nothing in life, but I was resolved that you should not enjoy what I had lost. Silvela, tonight the debits and credits of your account with me stand balanced. Across the page of the book of life I write the works, *'Paid in full!'"*

He heard me through. Then, as he realized that hope was gone, shriek after terrible shriek burst from his frenzied lips. In his terror and despair, he struggled in a madness of desperation; but every movement caused the embrace of the ghastly arms to tighten upon his body.

With a sick heart, I turned from the awful scene and plunged forward on my homeward path. As I passed around the great rock from where we had first glimpsed the fatal tree, a last heartbreaking wail reached my ears.

"Mercedes! Mercedes!"

Like the last cry of a lost soul hovering over the abyss of gehenna, it shrilled in vibrating terror through the air, echoing back from the ghoulish rocks, and then died away into the silence of the approaching night.

A faintness seized me, and I shivered at the touch of the chilling breeze which sprang up as the sun sank, blood-red, below the horizon: and my heart was as cold as my shrinking flesh.

Sunshine or shadow—it is the same to me now. But the recompense for my shattered life, I shall carry with me always, the vision of Silvela's distorted form writhing in close embrace of the devil-tree's snaky arms, in my ears there will ever ring the echo of his last despairing cry of, *"Mercedes!"*

The Purple Heart

The Story of a Haunted Cabin

HERMAN SISK

I was weary of the fog that hung over me like a pall, fatigued to the point of exhaustion. Since early afternoon the chill wind had forced it through my clothing like rain. It depressed me.

The country through which I had traveled alone was desolate and unpeopled, save here and there where some bush assumed fantastic form. The very air was oppressive. As far as I could see, were hills—nothing but hills and those bushes. Occasionally I could hear the uncanny cry of some hidden animal.

As I pushed on, a dread of impending disaster fastened itself upon me. I thought of my home, of my mother and sister, and wondered if all was well with them. I tried to rid myself of this morbid state of mind; but try as I would, I could not. It grew as I progressed, until as length it became a part of me.

I had walked some fifteen miles, and was so weary I could scarcely stand, when I came suddenly upon a log cabin. It was a crude affair, quite small, and stood back some distance from the little-used road in a clump of trees. A tiny window and a door faced the direction from which I approached. No paint had ever covered the roughly-hewn logs from which it was made, and the sun and the wind and the fog had turned the virgin wood to a drab brown.

I felt it was useless to knock, for the cabin had every appearance of being deserted. However, rap I did. No voice bade me enter, and with an effort I pushed open the door and staggered into the house. Almost immediately my weary legs crumpled under me, and I toppled and struck heavily on my face.

When I regained consciousness, a rough room, scantily furnished, greeted my eye. There was an ill-looking table, the top of which was warped and rectangular in shape, standing in the center. To one side was a rustic chair. Beyond the table was a bunk built into the wall; and on this lay a man with shining eyes and a long, white beard. A heavy gray blanket covered all of him but his head.

"You're right on time," he said in a high-pitched voice.

I looked at him closely.

"I don't know you," I said.

"Nor I you; but I knew you would come."

"You are ill and need help?" I asked.

"No," he replied in his strange monotone. "But on this day some one always visits here. None has ever returned. But I have yet to be alone on the night of this anniversary."

There was something so weird in the way he looked at me out of those big, watery eyes that I involuntarily shuddered.

"What anniversary?" I asked.

"The murder of my father," he answered. "It happened many years ago. A strange man came to this cabin just as you have done."

He paused. I said nothing.

"You wish to stay all night?" he asked.

"Yes, if I may," I replied. A moment later, I regretted it.

"Quite so," said he, with a slight nod of his white head. "Those were the very words he addressed to us. We took him in. When morning came I found my father dead in there," rolling his eyes and raising his head to indicate some point behind him, "with a dagger in his heart. You can see the room if you open the door behind me."

I looked at him a moment, hesitating. Then I went to the door and pushed it open. Cautiously glancing into the other room, I saw there was nothing there but a bunk similar to the one the old man occupied.

"Don't be afraid," he said, evidently sensing my fear. "Nothing will hurt you now. It's after midnight when it happens."

"What happens?" I asked.

"I don't know. No two men have the same experience. It all depends on one's state of mind."

"You mean—" I began.

"Yes," he interrupted. "One man saw hands reaching toward him and ropes in the air. He was escaping the gallows. Another saw faces of beautiful girls. He was on his way to a large church wedding. A third saw pools of blood and the white snow stained by human life. He was again living through a massacre in Russia."

"Do you live here?"

"No. No one does. The cabin is quite deserted. I come each year to welcome the evening's guest."

"Is there no other place to stay?" I asked, a sudden fear seizing me.

"None. Besides, it is growing dark without, and you would lose your way even if you could leave."

There was something ominous in the way he uttered these last five words.

"Yes," he went on, as if I had asked the unuttered question in my mind, "you may think you can go, but you cannot. That is the curse my father placed on this cabin. And I come each year to see that his word is obeyed. Whoever enters that door yonder on this date must stay until morning, and endure the agonies that only the rising sun can dispel."

I looked about me to make sure that he and I were the only living things in the room.

"What is to prevent my leaving?" I asked.

"Try to," he replied, an eerie note of glee in his queer voice.

I walked to the door and gave a mighty pull. To my utter amazement, it was locked!

I tried again, this time with greater determination; but the door remained unyielding. A sudden terror seized me. I turned to beseech the old man to let me go, but he was not there!

I looked quickly about me. He was nowhere to be seen. I ran into the other room. It was as empty as before. I rushed to the door there and pulled vigorously, but my efforts were in vain.

Returning to his bunk, I examined it closely. To my great astonishment, the heavy gray blanket was gone. In desperation I tried once more the door through which I had entered the cabin. It was still as inflexible as concrete.

Darkness fell fast and the room became very dim. I groped about and discovered some matches and a candle on a shelf under the table. I struck a match and lighted the candle. Letting some of the tallow drip onto the table, I made a stick for it. I then sat down on the edge of the bunk and anxiously awaited developments. But nothing occurred to mar the somber silence of my prison.

Thus I remained until my watch pointed to the hour of nine. My journey had greatly fatigued me, but my fears counterbalanced my weariness, so that I kept awake in spite of it.

At length, however, my eyelids grew heavy; my eyes became bleary, so that the candle multiplied, and my head drooped until my chin rested on my chest.

Letting the candle burn, I lay back on the hard bunk. I was cold and very nervous, and greatly felt the need of food and dry clothing. But my fatigue soon overcame me and I fell asleep.

When I awakened, a sense of suffocation and bewilderment hung over me. Whereas the room had been cold when I lay down, it now seemed close and hot. I pulled myself to a sitting posture. The room was dark. The candle was out.

I jumped to my feet and started toward the table. But in another moment I stood frozen to the spot, my eyes arrested and my body palsied by what I saw before me.

At the far end of the room was a purple glow in the shape of a human heart. It was stationary when I saw it, but almost immediately it began to move about the room. Now it was at the window. Then beside the table. Again it moved quickly but silently into the other room.

I pulled my frightened senses together and groped my way to the table. I found a match. With trembling hands, I struck it and lit the candle. To my surprise, it was almost as tall as when I had fallen asleep. I looked at my watch. It was one o'clock.

A moment later the flame was snuffed out and I was again in total darkness. I looked wildly about me. Horrors! The purple heart was beside me! I shrank back in terror. It came closer.

Suddenly I acquired superhuman courage. I grasped for the spectre. I touched nothing. I placed my left hand before me at arm's length. Lo! it was between me and my hand!

Presently it moved away. A great calm settled over me and I began to sense a presence in the room. Now, without any fear and with steady hand, I again struck a match and lighted the candle. It was promptly extinguished. I struck another with similar results.

And now something brushed my lips and an arm was passed lightly about my shoulders, but I was no longer afraid. The room continued cozily warm, and a greater sense of peace came over me.

Presently I lay down again and watched the purple heart as it came toward me and took its place at the edge of the bunk, like some loved one sitting beside me.

I must have fallen asleep again, for I knew no more until broad daylight awakened me, and I found myself lying in the middle of the room. There was no fog. The sun was shining brightly, and a broad beam was streaming through the dusty window pane. The candle and the matched were no longer visible.

Suddenly I thought of the locked door. Springing to it, I gave a mighty pull. It opened easily!

I snatched my cap from the rough floor and hurried into the warm sunlight.

A short distance from me a man came trudging along. He was a powerful looking fellow of middle age and was dressed in coarse working clothes.

"Do you know anything about that cabin?" I shouted, as we drew closer.

"Sure. It's haunted," he replied. He looked hard at me. "Were *you* in there last night?"

I related my experience.

"That's queer!" he muttered. "But I ain't surprised. Last night was the night."

"What night?" I demanded.

"Ten years ago an old man was murdered in that cabin, and his son swore on his deathbed he'd come back every anniversary and lure somebody into the cabin for the night and torture him."

He shuddered, his white face staring at the cabin.

"Come away!" he whispered. "Come away! It's haunted! It's haunted!"

JUNE 1923

Despite the presence of such key contributors as Otis Adelbert Kline and George Warburton Lewis, forgettable stories fill the fourth issue of *Weird Tales*, which also included one article, a short-lived feature by Preston Langley Hickey, "The Cauldron," and the perennial editorial column, "The Eyrie."

Seventeen stories comprise Volume I, Number 4, including the conclusion of A. G. Birch's "The Moon Terror," the first half of Paul Ellsworth Triem's "The Evening Wolves" and a reprint of Edgar Allan Poe's "The Murders in the Rue Morgue."

June 1923 also contains the third of five stories that Julian Kilman wrote for *Weird Tales* (all were published during the first year). At least three of Kilman's tales are so good that it was difficult for me to observe my longstanding "one entry per author" rule. I finally opted for "The Well" because I consider it the only story worth preserving from the fourth issue.

The Well

JULIAN KILMAN

Jeremiah Hubbard toiled with a team of horses in a piece of ground some distance down the road from his dwelling. When it neared five o'clock in the autumn afternoon, he unwound the lines from his waist, unhooked the traces and started home with his horses. He was a heavy man, a bit under middle age, with a dish-shaped face and narrow-set eyes. He walked with vigor. One of the horses lagged a trifle, and he struck it savagely with a short whip.

They came presently to the Eldridge dwelling, abandoned and tumbled down, on the opposite side of the road. The farm was being worked on shares by a man named Simpson, who lived five miles away and drove a "tin Lizzie." An ancient oak tree, the tremendous circumference of its trunk marred by signs of decay, reared splendid gnarled branches skyward.

These branches shaded a disused well — a well that had been the first one in Nicholas County, having been dug in the early fifties by the pioneering Eldridge family. It went forty feet straight down into the residual soil characteristic of the *locale*, but, owing to improved drainage, it had become dry. Nothing remained of the old pump-house, save the crumbling circle of stonework around the mouth, to give evidence of its one-time majesty.

A child of eight ran from the rear of the premises. Hubbard frowned and stopped his team.

"You better keep away from there," he growled, "or you'll fall into the well."

The girl glanced at him impishly.

"You an' Missus Hubbard don't speak to each other, do you?"

Hubbard's face went black. His whip sprang out and caught the girl about the legs. She yelped and ran.

An eighth of a mile farther along the road Hubbard turned in and drove his team to a big barn. He fed his stock. It was after six when he entered the house. This was a structure that, by comparison with the gigantic barn in the rear, seemed pigmy-like.

A sallow, flat-chested woman, with a wisp of hair twisted into a knot, took from Hubbard the two pails of milk he carried. She set them in the kitchen. The two exchanged no words.

Hubbard strode to the washstand, his boots thumping the floor, and performed his ablutions. He rumpled his hair and beard, using much soap and water and blowing stertorously. In the diningroom a girl of twelve sat with a book. As her father came in she glanced at him timorously.

He gave no heed to her as he slumped down into a chair standing before a desk, The desk was littered with papers, among which were typewritten sheets of the sort referred to as "pleadings"; there was a title-search much bethumbed and black along the edges, where the "set-outs" had been scanned with obvious care.

The man adjusted a pair of antiquated spectacles to his dish-face. To do this he was compelled to pull the ends over the ears as his nose afforded practically no bridge to support the glasses.

Presently he spoke to the girl:

"Tell your mother to bring on the supper."

The girl hastened out, and shortly thereafter the mother appeared carrying dishes. Food was disposed about the table in silence. The farmer ate gustily and in ten minutes finished his meal. Then he addressed his daughter, keeping his eyes averted from his wife. "Tell your mother," he said, "that I'll want breakfast at five o'clock tomorrow morning."

"Where you goin', Pa?" asked the girl.

"I'm goin' to drive to the county seat to see Lawyer Simmons."

Hubbard's gaze followed the girl as she helped clear the table.

"Look'a here." he said. "You been a-talkin' to that Harper child?"

"No," returned the daughter, with a trace of spirit. "But I jest saw her father over by the fence."

"What was he a-doin' there?"

"I didn't stay. I was afeared he'd catch me watchin' him."

Hubbard glowered and reached for his hat.

"I'll find out," he snarled.

Walking rapidly, he crossed a field of wheat stubble, keeping his eyes fixed sharply ahead. It was dusk, but presently, at the northern extremity of his premises, he made out the figure of a man.

"Hey, Harper!" he shouted. "You let that fence be."

He ran forward swiftly.

The men were now separated by two wire-strand fences that paralleled each other only three feet apart. These fences, matching one another for a distance of about two hundred yards—each farmer claiming title to the fence on the side farthest from his own—represented the basis of the litigation over the boundary claim that had gone on between them for four years.

The odd spectacle of the twin fences had come to be one of the show places in the county. It had been photographed and shown in agricultural journals.

"I don't trust ye, Harper," announced Hubbard, breathing hard. "You got the inside track with Jedge Bissell, an' the two of you are a-schemin' to beat me."

A laugh broke from the other.

"I'll beat you, all right," he said coolly. "But it won't be because Judge Bissell is unfair."

His manner enraged Hubbard, who rushed swiftly at the first fence and threw himself over. With equal celerity, he clambered over the second fence.

Startled by the sudden outburst of temper, Harper had drawn back. He held aloft a spade. Hubbard leaped at him. The spade descended.

Harper was slightly-built, however, and the force of the blow did not halt the infuriated man, now swinging at him with all his might. They clinched. Hubbard's fingers caught at the throat of the smaller man, and the two stumbled to the ground, Hubbard atop. The fall broke his grip. With his huge fists he began to hammer the body. He continued until it was limp.

Then, his rage suddenly appeased, he drew back and stared at the inert figure lying strangely quiet.

"So!" he gasped.

There came the sound of someone singing, the voice floating distinctly through the night air. Hubbard recognized it for that of an itinerant Free Methodist minister, whose church in Ovid he and his family occasionally attended.

The song rolling forth, as the Man of God drove along the highway in his rig, was Jesus, Lover of My Soul.

For the moment, Hubbard shielded his face with an arm as if to ward off an invisible thing.

Then, bending over the prostrate form, he ran his hand inside the clothing to test the action of the heart. He performed the act mechanically, because he knew he had killed his man.

He discovered the handbag. Evidently Harper was on his way to Ovid to catch the train to the county seat for the trial on the morrow. This meant that he would not be missed by his wife for at least twenty-four hours.

The murderer studied his next move. Where to secrete the body? A piece of wood lay back of him, but he was aware that it was constantly combed by squirrel hunters. He thought of the railroad. Why not an accident? Killed by the very train he was bound for?

He started to lug the body toward the track which passed half a mile to the north. Realizing, however, that for the time at hand the distance was too great, he let the body slide to the ground. Next he stole along the twin fences to the highway and peered both ways. No one seemed abroad.

He came back on the dead run, and in twenty minutes he had carried the body to the Eldridge premises and flung it town the ancient well.

When he returned he found his wife and daughter together in the parlor, where with the itinerant preacher, all three were kneeling on the floor in prayer. Hubbard unceremoniously nudged the clergyman.

"That'll do," he said.

The minister rose, his tall, lanky figure towering over Hubbard.

"Brother," he began, in an orotund voice, "come with the Lord—"

"Yes, I know," returned Hubbard, with a patience that surprised his wife. "But I've got something to talk over with my family." He paused. "Here," he added, feeling in his pocket and producing a small coin, "take this and go along."

When the preacher had left, Hubbard called to his daughter.

"Harper was gone when I got over to the fence."

"What kept you so long?"

"I walked over to the woods. There's a nest of coons. They're a-goin' to play havoc with the corn." He smiled unnaturally. "Look a-here! If we can catch 'em, I'll give you the money their pelts bring."

Hubbard divined that his acting was poor. Both the girl and his wife were frankly regarding him.

"Well!" he shouted. "What's the matter with ye?"

"Oh, nuthin' Pa, nuthin'" whimpered the girl.

"Then go to bed, the two of ye."

Next morning Hubbard started for the county seat, a ten mile drive. He returned that evening and complained that the case had been adjourned because Harper had failed to appear in court.

The following day he went back to his field far down the road for more ploughing. Twice he was called to the roadside by passersby to discuss the disappearance of Harper.

One morning a week later, when he came along the road with his team, he discovered the Harper child on the Eldridge premises. She was sitting at the edge of the well.

With a surprised oath, he dropped the lines and half-walked, half-ran, to where the girl sat.

"Didn't I tell you to stay away from there!" he exploded.

The girl stared at him, but made no move, though her lips quivered. Hubbard glanced back to observe the road. Then he caught her arm.

"Go home!" he shouted.

He spun her roughly. She continued to stare at him as she retreated homeward.

All that morning, Hubbard worked his horses hard. He realized that he was eager to go back by the Eldridge dwelling. Promptly at twelve o'clock, therefore, he tied his team and started up the road. A flash of relief came to him when he did not observe the little girl. It left him cold, however.

"Eatin' dinner," he mumbled.

He moved off, without looking into the well. Until four o'clock that afternoon he labored. On his way home he discovered the girl again seated by the well. She was bending over and acting queerly.

Hurrying his horses to the roadside, he looped the lines over one of the posts in the old "snake" fence. As he approached, he saw her toss a piece of stone down the hole.

Hubbard waited until he was sure of his voice.

"Come with me," he said.

Gripping the girl he started with her toward her home but a short distance away. When they arrived the front door was ajar. A woman, with eyes red from weeping, looked at Hubbard in silence.

"Here!" he said gruffly. "This child ought to be kept to home. She'll fall into the well."

Mrs. Harper merely reached out her arms for her daughter. Hubbard remained standing awkwardly.

"Have you heard anything of Harper yet?" he asked.

"I don't want to talk to you," replied the woman.

Hubbard turned on his heel. Waiting for him by his horses, was the deputy sheriff. The two further discussed the disappearance.

"If you yourself wasn't so well known, Jeremiah," finally declared the official, "they'd sure be thinkin' you was in it some way."

"Why!" grunted the farmer, as he untied the lines.

"Well, everybody known you an' Harper been lawin' it for years over that boundary line."

Hubbard achieved a laugh.

"I'll tell ye where Harper is. He's cleared out, that's what I think—deserted his family."

That night, and many following nights, Hubbard did not sleep. Some weeks later a tremendous electric storm broke in the night. One particularly heavy clap so startled the wakeful Hubbard that he leaped from his bed and dressed. In the pouring rain he started out.

Inevitably his steps took him toward the well. It was black, and he could not see at first. But another flash came, and he observed a strange thing:

The huge oak, standing at the side of the well, had split in two by lightning, and one portion of the tree and fallen over the mouth of the hole.

Next morning Simpson, the man with the "tin Lizzie," stopped by at Hubbard's place. He was a blunt-spoken, red-faced man whom Hubbard hated.

"That was a bad storm last night." he said. "The lightning struck the big oak tree by the well."

"What of it?" snapped Hubbard.

"There was a skeleton in the center of that tree, "explained Simpson. "I was talking this morning with the sheriff over the telephone. He said seventy-five years ago a man was murdered in Ovid, and they never found his body. This skeleton must be his."

Hubbard cleared his throat sharply.

"What did you do with it?"

"The skull and one of the leg bones fell down into the well when I tried to gather them up. I want to borrow some rope so I can get down in there."

For a bare second Hubbard was silent.

"What you ought to do," he said, gathering himself, "is to fill up that hole. It's dangerous."

"Yes. That's so. But I'm goin' to get that skull first. It'll be a good exhibit. I'm wonderin' whether we'll ever find Harper's skeleton."

"Wait a moment," said Hubbard huskily, starting for the barn. "I'll get some rope and help you."

The two returned to the Eldridge farm. They found there the dead man's child. She had perched herself on the fallen tree.

"Damn fool!" muttered Hubbard. "Her mother lettin' her play around here!"

A pulley was rigged over the branch and inserted with a board for a rest.

"I'll go down," vouchsafed Hubbard.

Simpson looked his surprise as he assented.

It took Hubbard five minutes or so to retrieve the missing skeleton parts. He brought them up, the leg bone and the grinning skull. He was pale when he hauled himself over the edge.

"I'm a-goin' to fill up that hole myself," he said.

"All right," retorted Simpson, handling the skull curiously. "Go to it."

Word traveled of the finding of the skeleton, and the inhabitants began driving thither to see the sight. Simpson, a man of some ingenuity, had wired the bleached white bones together and suspended them from one of the branches of the fallen tree. The skeleton dangled and swung in the wind.

Hubbard, maddened by the delay and publicity, felt himself wearing away. He had become obsessed with conviction that if the hole were filled his mind would be at rest.

The nights of continued sleeplessness were ragging his nerves, and he was by this time unable to remain in bed. He would throw himself down, fully dressed, waiting until the others were asleep. Then he would steal out.

At first he had merely walked the roads, swinging his arms and mumbling. But as the night progressed his stride would quicken, and frequently he would take to running. He would run until his lungs were bursting and a slaver fed from his mouth. Late travelers began to catch glimpses of the fleeting figure, and the rumor grew that a ghost was haunting the locality of the well—that the skeleton walked.

Hubbard grew haggard. But he found himself unable to continue his nocturnal prowls, some of which took him miles, but all of which invariably wound up at one place — the well.

Here, fagged and exhausted, he would sit until the approach of dawn, staring at the swinging skeleton, mouthing incoherencies, praying, singing hymns beneath his breath, laughing. At the approach of dawn he would steal home.

At last, after interest in the skeleton had subsided and Simpson had consented to its removal, Hubbard loaded his wagon with stones and small boulders and started for the well. That first forenoon he mane three trips, dumping each time a considerable quantity of stones.

Next morning he worked in an additional trip. He began to experience surcease. But on the afternoon of the second day, when he made another trip, Simpson came over from his work in an adjoining field.

"I wanted to see you yesterday," he said, quizzically regarding Hubbard. "Mrs. Harper was here. She said her little girl was playin' around here and dripped a pair of andirons down the well."

"What of it?" Hubbard jerked out.

"You got to get 'em out."

"Why?"

"Because them andirons is relics."

"But you gave me permission to fill the hole."

"I was kiddin' you," laughed Simpson. "I'm only rentin' the farm. I ain't got nothin' to do with the house and yard."

Without a word Hubbard turned to his wagon. He got into the seat and drove off. In an hour he came back with the same rope that had been used to recover the missing portions of the skeleton. Also, he brought with him a farm laborer who did occasional work for him.

Simpson regarded Hubbard amusedly as the latter adjusted once more the pulley, arranged a bucket and then hitched his team to the end of the rope.

Patiently, bucketful by bucketful, the stones were elevated and dumped. Down below in the black interior, Hubbard labored for an hour. At six o'clock he had not found the andirons. Twice he had been compelled to come up for fresh air.

His last trip up left him so white-faced and weak that he was forced to go home.

That night he resorted to sleeping powders. But he lay and tossed, wide-eyed through the dark hours. Sometime after midnight he got up. A light was still burning in his wife's room, and, tiptoeing down the hall, he paused at her door. In low voices the mother and daughter were conversing. To his heated imagination it seemed certain they were talking of Harper's disappearance.

Mumbling to himself he left the house. He ran down the lane to the highway and along this until he came to the Eldridge place. He determined not to stop, and succeeded in running by, like a frightened animal.

His gait accelerated. It was one best described as scurrying, as he ran crouched and low. He thought he saw someone approaching. This turned him. Back he fled with the speed of the wind.

Drawn by an irresistible force, he made straight for the Eldridge pathway. He came to the well, the entrance of which gaped at him. For a moment he stood, with eyes wide open, staring into the black depths.

Then, screaming, he plunged in head-first.

His cry, long-drawn and eerie, hung quivering on the night air.

In the Hubbard home, a quarter of a mile away, the mother and daughter heard it. The two listened with palpitating hearts. They caught one another's hands.

In a hoarse whisper, the mother exclaimed:

"What's that?"

JULY-AUGUST 1923

Financial problems plagued *Weird Tales* throughout its "revenant" existence and the first year was no exception. The publishers cut corners by making the next issue represent two months.

July-August 1923, designated Volume II, Number 1, is historically significant because Clark Ashton Smith's byline first appears in it. A personal friend of H. P. Lovecraft's and one of The Unique Magazine's most popular writers, Smith contributed two mediocre poems, "The Red Moon" and "The Garden of Evil."

Besides an article on voodoo and the second of Preston Langley Hickey's "The Cauldron," the fifth issue contains the end of the preceding issue's two-parter, the first half of the latest serial and fourteen other stories, including disappointing entries by Vincent Starrett and J. Paul Suter, whose earlier *Weird Tales* pieces were much better.

Pickings in this issue are slim. I have selected the novelette, "The Two Men Who Murdered Each Other," by Valma Clark, although my friend and colleague *Weird Tales* historian Bob Weinberg doesn't think much of it. But despite an improbable plot, I like its evocative style and feel that Clark's language comes closer to the spirit of poetry than the doggerel verse usually printed in *Weird Tales*.

The Two Men who Murdered Each Other

VALMA CLARK

It was on Cape Cod one August, while I was browsing through antique shops in quest of a particular kind of colonial andirons for one of our patrons, that I stumbled onto the Old Scholar. There, in a white farmhouse back from the King's Highway, among a litter of old Cape lanterns and great bulging liqueur bottles of green and amber glass, ancient teakettles and brass door knockers and the inevitable bayberry candles, I came upon painted book ends of heavy wood on which bright orange nymphs disported themselves against a velvet-black background. A bizarre color scheme, was my first conventional reaction.

Yet the details of face and hair were traced most delicately in brown and purple, as though a brush with a single fine bristle had been used; the work was exquisite, and on the whole the effect was charming. Then it struck me: Jove, it was after the manner of the old, fine, red-figured Greek vases—classic, that was it!

The nymphs, too, were classic; this slim one was, without doubt, Nausicaa playing at ball with her maidens. There were other classical subjects: a graceful Aphrodite riding a quaintly stiff swan; nimble sileni frolicking on a seesaw . . .

Pagan mythology running riot, within a small space, in this home of New England antiques—it was at least odd! Here, where one sought the genuine old colonial—though usually in vain, to be sure—to come upon this curious classical twist!

Even as I wondered, my eye fell upon a fresh subject, and the wonder changed to genuine admiration and sharpened to a very keen curiosity concerning the artist who achieved such arresting beauty with such crude materials. It was a broken painting, like a Venus with a missing arm. It showed the head and shoulders of Pallas Athena and the head and shoulders of a youth who played to her on a double flute. The goddess' head, which still bore the warrior's helmet, was bent in a listening attitude toward the music, and her pose was one of relaxation and peace after fierce combat.

67

It was a quiet thing, with quiet, flowing lines, for all the unfinished ragged edge which cut the figures off just above the waist. Somehow, it held the dignity and sincerity of great religious art. And now I noticed that there were other identical Athenas, that the fragmentary painting recurred on fully half the book ends: as though it were the motif of all his work, I thought—the one serious theme running through all these lighter themes.

"But only a man thoroughly steeped in Greek mythology—loving it—could do that —"

"Pardon, sir?" said the young woman who kept shop.

"This! It's rather remarkable. Who is he—tell me about him!" I begged of her impulsively.

"I can't tell you much. He lives alone over on the back shore, and he brings us these to sell. His name is Twining—'Tinker' Twining, they call him."

"But this broken thing—what does it mean?"

She shook her head.

"He never talks; only say he hasn't the pattern for the rest, and it would be sacrilege to finish it without the true lines."

"Hm—reverence and a conscience," I muttered. "Rare enough these days. I'll take the pair of them. How much?"

"Five dollars."

"And a pair of the nymphs," I added, since it seemed absurdly cheap.

"Sorry, but we've only one of these. It's used as a door prop, you see."

"No, not a *door prop!*" I lamented. "But I'd use mine as book ends, and I'd put the Romantic Poets between them."

"I'll tell you —" the girl turned suddenly helpful—"you might leave an order with us for Mr. Twining to paint you one. He'd be glad to do it."

"Or I might take the order to Mr. Twining myself," I exclaimed eagerly. "I've a car outside and I've time to kill. How do I get to him?"

"But you can't drive. You follow the sand road to the end, and then take a narrow path across to the ocean side. It's three miles over, the only house —"

"No matter! I've a fancy to meet him. Oh, I see by your face you wouldn't advise it."

"It's only that he's—something of a hermit," she hesitated. "He's a very courteous old gentleman, but no one ever visits him."

"Then it's time someone started, and I've a faculty for getting on with hermits," I assured her gaily.

I thanked her, found a quiet inn, parked my car for the night, and started on a late afternoon ramble for the back shore and a Mr. "Tinker" Twining.

II

I followed a sand trail like a wind-white chalk line between growths of springy hog cranberry, scrub oak and pine—a most desolate and forsaken country—until at last I stepped out abruptly upon a high cliff over the Atlantic Ocean.

Clouds had sponged out the blue sky, and instead of the late sunlight there was a strange yellow glow over everything. All those light, bright Cape colors—turquoise blue and gay copper-gold and honey-yellow—had been dimmed.

The sea was very still, of dull purples and greens, and the broad cream beach, below the sand scrap upon which I stood, had a grayish tinge. Above me, on the highest point of the cliff and huddled too close to its shifting edge, was one of those low, weather-beaten Cape houses. I climbed to it, and wading through beach grass and vines of the wild beach pea, came to the back door.

The house was quiet, and I had a glimpse of a scrupulously neat, old-style kitchen—cumbersome flatirons in a row and a brick oven built into the chimney—as I stood there hesitating.

Then, against a further window which framed the lowering sea and sky, I saw the profile of an old, white-haired man.

He sat at a work bench and he held a brush poised in his hand, but he was not painting. His head was up and he was listening—it was almost as though he were listening to that strange electric-yellow that permeated all the air, was the queer thought I had. I was struck at once by the extreme delicacy and the fine-drawn suffering of the old man's face; indeed, the lines of that tragic profile might have been traced with the single fine bristle of his own brush, in those same delicate browns and purples.

Moreover, the setting was all wrong: the old, frail face was somehow not up to that sullen sweep of sky and ocean. It was as though an exquisite thing of beaten and fretted silver should be mounted alone upon a coarse expanse of dull burlap—a broad background that called for granite at least.

I tapped, and the old man stirred.

"Good afternoon," I called.

He came slowly to the door.

"They sent me from that antique place—the *Open Latch*. I'd like to get you to do me another book end."

"Book end?" he muttered.

"I hoped you might be willing to paint it and send it on to me."

"Ah, yes." Clearly he was following me only with his eyes; with his soul he was still listening to his own thoughts.

I found myself puzzled as to how to reach him. A baffling aroma of archaism hung about this elderly man: breathed not only from his worn black suit, which was not of this day, but also from his manner and the very inflection of his voice, which were somehow reminiscent of the old school.

"The nymphs," I insisted, "the one of Nausicaa."

There I caught him. "Nausicaa—you knew?"

"Well, I guessed."

"They don't as a rule; in the general they are merely odd little maidens sporting at ball." His smile came out as pure gold filtered from the dross of suffering—a rare, lovable smile that immediately won me to the old gentleman. "I shall be happy to paint the Nausicaa for you, sir," he added formally, and awaited my further pleasure.

"The name," I said. "Perhaps you'd better jot down my name and address."

"Of course—the name." Obediently he brought pad and pencil, and in a fine, scholarly hand wrote "Mr. Claude Van Nuys," with my New York address.

Absently, he permitted me to pay him and stood ready to bid me good afternoon.

Still I lingered. "The sileni; and the goddess on the swan—Aphrodite, isn't she?"

"You pass, my boy—grade A," he smiled.

"And the Pallas Athena—that's splendid work, only why—?"

"Ah, the Athena!" A flicker of pain touched the old man's face, and he grew reticent and vague again.

I would have given him up then, had not a terrific and absolutely unheralded blast of wind come to my assistance, striking up the sand in swirling clouds about us.

"Whew!" I whistled, covering my face against the cut of that fine shot. "We're in for a gale, yes? I say —"

But I was shocked to dumbness by the look of strained and unadulterated horror on old Mr. Twining's face. He was breathing hard and backing into the house as though driven against the storm.

"A bad night," he muttered. "Wind and a sea . . . It was just such a night —" He rediscovered me with a start and with something approaching relief, I thought.

"But you couldn't stay out in this," he reasoned, more to himself than to me. "It then becomes necessary—Sir,"—he slipped easily into the role of courteous host—"will you accept the shelter of my roof until the storm passes?"

He waited for me to precede him into the house, saw me seated in the only comfortable chair in the dim living room, and, having first excused himself, sat down at his work bench and again took up his brush.

Slowly the room darkened. The old man forgot me and relapsed into mutterings, quivering under each shrill onslaught of the wind, pausing to listen for the moan of the surf below.

"You're deucedly close to this cliff," I ventured once, when a shower of sand swished against the window-pane.

"Eh—the cliff? Some winter nights she'll rise up to the very house and drench the glass of my windows—the sea will," he shuddered. "She's eating back—eating back; forty years ago, when I first came here, there was a front yard."

"But isn't it unsafe?"

"Perhaps," vaguely.

So he worked on until he could no longer see, and then he lit a candle, and turned to the tracing of a pattern from the colored plate of a book. There were several similar volumes at his elbow, and I dared to take one up and run it through. They were, as I had guessed, plates of the more famous Greek vases—mostly those of the red-figured period. "Douris—Euphronios—Hieron," I read aloud. "Oh, and those exquisite old white lekythoi!"

The effect upon the old man was instantaneous. Those names — *Hieron, white lekythoi*—were the magic passwords to him! He turned to me as a starved dog might turn to food:

"Ah, you know them—the cup-painters!" And he loosed upon me such a flood of scientific enthusiasm and technicalities and dates, with such an undercurrent of reverence and love for the pure beauty of these old vases, as left me breathless, feeling that I had at last found a scientist and a poet rolled into one.

"You know, you know!" he exulted. "Now you recall the Douris Athena —"

"But I know nothing, really," I interrupted him, impelled to honesty by his own intense sincerity. "My knowledge of the classics is general. We deal only in period stuff at the House of Harrow, where I'm a buyer—English and French periods mostly—for a Fifth Avenue clientele. Oh, I once dipped into Greek art on my own account, picked up the patter, but beyond that —"

He would not have it.

"You speak the language," he insisted. "And do you know that it is nearly half a century since I've met a man who's ever heard of Euphronios, the master cup-painter? Lord, how it takes me back!"

The old man laughed. The storm and his terrors were forgotten; the glow in his heart burned up in his cheeks like a fever.

"This—these books,"—his hand swept the colored plate — "they're all I have left—the only link I allow myself."

"Do you mean—? With your passion for the classics, you shut yourself up alone here—starve yourself! But in God's name, man, why?"

"That's why—in God's name." The old man's head was bowed; for a moment the pain was back on his face. But that brittle zest flamed up in him again. "You questioned about my Athena! You are the first man who would comprehend. Wait!"

Smiling like a child with a secret, he tiptoed to a chest of drawers, brought out something wrapped in tissue paper. Very tenderly he unwound the papers, and produced before me the broken half of a red-figured cylix, with one handle attached but with the standard missing. He waited triumphantly for my exclamation.

"Why," I said lamely, "the interior is that same Athena with her flute player. It seems—a very fine fragment —"

"Fine!"—he scorned the adjective. "Fine? Sir, this is the best of its kind—the aristocrat of the Greek vase. See!—The finished lines went something like this."

He caught up a pencil, laid the fragment flat on a sheet of white paper, and completed the broken figures of the Athena and the youth.

I noted his hands as he sketched: fine, long-fingered hands, nervous, but sure at their work.

"You see?" he asked. "Now on the exterior of the cylix we have Athena mounting her quadriga after the battle. Is it not a contrast, that peaceful Athena and this Athena? Is he not, indeed, an artist of variety, the man who could do those two things, each so perfectly? You will note the horses—the bold, vigorous lines—the power and swing. It is naked, masculine drawing this—yes, scriptural. Euphronios —" Old Twining broke off, returned to his more precise exposition: "The other half of the cup—the exterior—showed Athena sending her spear into the giant Ankelados —"

"But where is the other half?" I wondered. "You must have seen it, since you hold the answer to the riddle."

"Yes," he returned slowly, "I have seen it; God knows I do hold the answer to the riddle . . ."

But he came back to me—or rather to the beloved fragment of the cylix.

"The coloring!" he breathed. "That deep orange glow and the velvet black and that fine gloss over all . . . The secret of Greek potters, buried with them. Perfect to the very eyelashes . . ."

Sitting there, he lost himself in reverent admiration of the shard. He did not touch it—it was as though the fragment were too precious to handle; but he gave his soul to it through his eyes. He was oblivious to the wail of a rising wind and the thunder of a rising surf.

"It is," he announced quietly at last, "the half of a genuine, unpublished Euphronios."

I stared. "You say this is—an unpublished Euphronios?"

"Yes. The signature was on the other piece."

"But man alive, given that other piece—and you must know where it is to be so familiar with it—this fragment is worth a king's ransom. A genuine whole Euphronios—why, the museums alone, bidding against each other —"

"The other half is gone," spoke the old man, "gone forever. But this piece itself is still worth more than a king's ransom; not in gold, but in the coin of knowledge—the knowledge it will give the world of Greek art."

His gray eyes wandered to a vision; the poet was drowned in the farseeing scientist.

For that instant I felt myself in the presence of nobility

— but the old man's dignity was abruptly shattered. With the rush as of an oncoming engine, the full blast of an Atlantic gale struck us: screamed and whined and groaned, and shook the old house until it rattled like a bag of loose bones.

In the same moment the rain came down in a deluge, swept the window-panes and beat a very devil's tattoo upon the roof. I flatter myself I am no coward, but I found myself clutching at the heavy work bench for anchorage. By the wavering candlelight I discovered my host pressed to his eyes. He seemed to be in physical agony; it flashed to me that he was suffering a stroke of some kind.

I reached him in two steps: "What is it? Sir—Mr. Twining!"

His mutterings were part of a disjointed prayer. I laid my hand on his shoulder, and suddenly he was clinging to me, like a child who finds an unexpected hand in the dark, and was speaking rapidly, incoherently: "No, no, it's not the storm; it's the things it brings up here, in my head—images—scenes no human being should have . . . staged. I live it over again—over and over—like Macbeth. Don't leave me—don't! It's His will. He sends you, and the storm holds you here—impossible for you to reach the village this night. You shall stay with me, be my first guest in forty years. You shall hear my tale—and judge me."

"Yes, yes," I soothed him, drawing him to a chair, "of course I'll stay."

III

He subsided then, his head dropped to his arms which he had flung out on the bench before him; as the wind died down a little, he slowly regained complete control of himself.

"It's mad of me," he sighed, facing me at last. "Sometimes I fear I am growing a little mad. But I've a fancy to tell to you — an impartial stranger—the story of how I came by the Euphronios fragment. But you must be hungry; you shall first have supper with me."

He became again the solicitous but unobtrusive host. He moved expertly about the kitchen, set a meticulous table with white linen cloth and pewter utensils, and served me clam broth out of a blue bowl, and brown bread and honey, and some sort of flower wine of which Horace might have sung. The old man himself supped on three steamed clams and a glass of cold water. Yet he was the perfect host with his fine, aloof hospitality.

At last we settled to the story. Sitting there on opposite sides of his work bench, with the storm rising and falling in intermittent gusts, and with the broken fragment of the vase between us, its colors glowing out like black onyx and orange coral under the sputtering light of the candle, we dropped back into the old man's past:

"I was abroad," he began, "in the middle of the eighties, on a year's leave of absence from my college, and with me was my friend—Lutz, let us call him—Paul Lutz. I may say here that I had no right to play friend to him, for at heart I despised him—despised his methods, his creeds. One of my college colleagues, a younger man than I, he seemed to have taken a liking to me.

"It was odd, for he was of a wealthy family, and beyond our common interest in archeology and classical subjects—an interest which was rather a fad with him, I suspected—we were at opposite poles. He was shrewd, brilliant even, but how shall I describe him—he had thick fingers. He was the handsome, spoiled, Byronic type: a full-blooded dark man, part Jewish. I have sometimes wondered if I did not keep him by me to watch him, for we were rivals in the same field, even in the same little department, and in those days I made finger exercises of the theories of other scholars and dreamed of striking a great new chord of my own. I wanted fame, you see, recognition, and I was suspicious of Lutz's brilliance. I dare say the basis of many apparent friendships in this world in really a strong rivalry and a mutual suspicion.

"Lutz and I were rivals in more ways than one. There was . . . a young lady in our college town; she received us both. Her name—it would do no harm to tell it now—was Lorna Story, and she was like her name, a fine, silver-gray girl. She had a beautiful mind . . . and a light shining through her gray eyes that was like the haunting line of a poem . . ."

The old man sat silent for a time, as he had been silent before the fine beauty of his Greek vase, and his old, frail face was lit by the same inner glow. He moved to take up from the base of the candlestick a hurt night moth, and, cupping it gently in his two hands, opened the window a crack and released it. Then he continued:

"Lutz and I were in Athens together in the spring in the interest of our college museum, which was then in its infancy. We had at our joint disposal a fund for any valuable specimens, and we haunted the excavation fields and the markets for antiquities. It was the merest chance which led us to the Acropolis at the time they had just started on the work of clearing out the debris which dated before the destruction of the Persians. And it was the merest chance which took us to the spot at the moment the workmen brought to light the vase, in two pieces.

"A vase by the potter Euphronios—and the signature was actually visible through the coating of white earth deposits—here in this debris which went back to the days before the Persian sacking in 480! Now Euphronios had long been fixed at a date considerably later. That difference in dates was important: the inferences that followed—why, I had hit upon a tremendous, an epoch-making discovery! I saw my path to scholarly fame opening up before me.

"I talked with the young Greek who was directing operations there, and secured his promise that I should examine the specimen when it had been thoroughly cleaned. Lutz edged close to me, and I saw that he, too, was excited by the vase, though concealing his excitement under an air of indifference. But I had no time for Lutz. I got away from him. I pursued those inferences for miles through the streets of Athens, and then tested out my conclusions in the classical library out at the American School. There was no error in my facts, no flaw in my logic.

"I walked the streets longer—hours longer—bit by bit built up my article. Then, in the flush of masterly achievement, I turned back to the small hotel where we were stopping.

"I opened the door of our room to find Lutz bent low over the table. He was gloating over something: "You beauty! And to fit with never a flaw—'

" 'Good Lord!' I discovered. 'It's the vase!'

" 'Right, old boy," Lutz grinned up at me. 'I've finished giving her a bath with aqua fortis—oh, my caution was extreme, never fear. Now what do you think?'

"Think! What could I think? The colors were as you see them now, startling, like black and orange enamel. Forgetful of theories, I fell into rhapsodies with him. Lutz caressed the glossy, painted surface with his plump hands and fairly purred; I darted from the tracery of face and garments to the Greek letters of the signature and sipped the honey of our rare find after my own fashion.

"We were like two eager boys who have come upon Captain Kidd's treasure. We dropped into heated argument, I recall: Lutz preferred the strong, battling Athena who hurled her spear at the giant, while I maintained that the quiet Athena, who sat with her head bowed to the music of her flute player was the greater art. Laughingly, I took possession of my favorite half of the vase and left Lutz to his savage goddess.

"Then the serious significance of the vase and my intended article intruded, and I returned to earth. " 'But how under heaven did you come by it, Lutz?'

"He laughed, cast an apprehensive glance toward the hallway: 'It's a long story. I say, will you lock that door behind you? Thanks. Whether that Greek was a fool that he should let this slip through his fingers, or whether it was a question of drachmas or whether it was a little of both—idiocy and greed — what does it matter? The vase is here—mine. Well, then—'

" 'But it belongs by right to the Greek government—the Museum of the Acropolis,' I protested, weakly enough.

" 'Naturally, I know.' He smiled. 'But it does not go to the Greek government, nor to the Acropolis. Now why quibble, Twining? You know these things are done every day.'

"I did know: in spite of laws, valuable classical pieces were continually turning up in the States; indeed, our own college had purchased specimens of doubtful past.

" 'How much, then?'

" 'Guess!' And he named a sum that startled me.

" 'It's a lot,' I grumbled. 'And look here, Lutz, I expect to be consulted at least in the disposal of the fund. Still, anything within reason for it . . . a superb nucleus of our collection. . .' Then the thrill of my discovery caught me again: 'Its value is greater than you realize, Lutz. You saw nothing strange in finding a vase by Euphronios in the Persian rubbish? Why, wake up, man! If Euphronios and his contemporaries lived and painted before the Persians, it simply means that the whole chronology of Greek vases must be pushed back half a century. And that's going to mean that Greek painting developed before Greek sculpture, instead of the contrary, as we've always believed. Now do you see! Do you begin to see how this one small vase is going to revolutionize all of our concepts of Greek art? Why, it's colossal! When my article appears—when it's published and quoted and discussed and rediscussed in all the periodicals—'

" 'Hold on!' commanded Lutz. 'We'll not make a splurge of this vase yet. You'll hang off on that article a while—promise me?'

" 'I don't follow you,' I returned, stiffening. 'Why should I make promises—?'

" 'But I insist that you shall!'

" 'And I reply that I won't!'

"Lutz's black eyes narrowed, his face tightened to an expression of hard shrewdness. 'As I see it, your theory depends upon your establishing the fact that the vase came out of that Persian junk; unless you can guarantee that, the whole theory goes smash. I think you'll find no one who'll swear to that. You'd have to swear to it alone. And if it came to a showdown, it would be your one word against our several words. Since the thing you're trying to prove is contrary to accepted ideas, the public would find it easier to believe us.'

" 'But the vase was taken from the Persian debris; you yourself saw it, this very morning!'

" 'Perhaps.'

" 'Yet you would—lie?'

" 'Perhaps.'

" 'But why? Can't you grasp it? It means,' I reiterated patiently, 'a big discovery concerning Greek art, and Greek art is the basis of other arts. You wouldn't keep that knowledge from the world? Oh, you're afraid of losing—but whether the vase goes to a Greek museum or to our museum, is nothing compared to the fact it will establish. You simply don't understand!'

" 'It's you,' said Lutz softly, 'who misunderstands. Did I neglect to tell you that I paid for the vase with a check on my own bank?'

" 'You didn't draw on the fund?'

" 'No.'

" 'Why—what—?'

" 'So you see, old top, you haven't been getting me quite straight: this cylix is *my* find!'

" 'What do you mean?'

"He colored then, beneath his dark skin. 'It's not for the college museum; it's for—my own private museum. I mean to make it the start of the very finest private collection in the States.' He held out his hand for my half of the cup.

"But I drew back, hugged the fragment against my breast. 'Do you stand there and tell me that you're not a scientist at all, but a greedy sensualist? You will remember, Lutz, that you're here for the college, sent by the college—'

" 'And I've worked like the devil for the college!' he broke in roughly. 'I'll continue to work for the college through all the regular channels. But this thing's not regular; it's most—irregular; and the irregularity is my own doing. I'll keep this vase for myself, and I'll suffer my own damnation for it. If you'll kindly hand over that piece—'

"Then I flared: 'I'll do nothing of the sort. If you think you can gag me to silence—force me to sit still and blink at your dirty greed—No, I'll keep this half as guarantee to us both that you'll see the light of day and do the right thing!'

"We had it hot, then. He had paid for it with his own money, had not touched a penny of the college fund; he had me there.

"But I swore, if he insisted upon taking the fragment from me, that I should report him to Greek authorities who watched that no Greek treasures should go from the country without government sanction.

"That held him. He desisted, even tried to square himself with me. Probably Lutz merely delayed the issue until we should be safely out of Greece. For myself, I was firmly resolved that I should finally prevail upon him; and I did not doubt that I should publish my article and either return the vase to Greece or hand it over to my college museum.

"Meantime, we sailed for home, taking passage, as we had planned, on a small trading vessel that wound a leisurely circle about the Atlantic islands and certain South American ports before it brought up and dropped anchor in New York Bay. The truce still held. Each of us guarded jealously his half of the vase, and each kept aloof from the other.

"It was a childish situation. I tried to tell myself that he was only a willful, spoiled boy, acting in character, but my secret hatred of him grew out of all proportion to the quarrel, which was serious enough, truly.

IV

"There was an implicit understanding between us that the reckoning would come when the ship landed us on home soil. But the ship was destined not to land.

"We were in mid-Atlantic, some eight hundred miles off the Cape Verde Islands and bound for Porto Seguro, when the crash came. It was night, with a heavy gale blowing, and at first I thought the sudden wrench which almost jerked me from my upper berth was a particularly violent wave. Then a grinding and shuddering through all the ship's frame and an abrupt cessation of the engine's throbbing, pulled me stark awake. I hung over the edge of my birth:

" 'What is it?'

" 'Don't know,' yawned Lutz below, struggling from luxurious sleep. 'Better find out—what? 's a damn nuisance—'

"I groped for the light, and we got into clothes, the ship pitching now so that it was impossible to keep a footing. We spoke no further word, but Lutz paused in drawing on his trousers to take from beneath his pillow the box which contained his half of the precious vase; and I reached for my own piece, and kept it by me while I finished lacing my shoes. Each of us eyed the other suspiciously; and Lutz was quick to follow me when, with my treasure, I mounted to the ship's deck.

"The little boat wallowed there in the trough of the sea, a dead and passive thing. With its heart stilled, it seemed strangely aloof from the wild sounds of the storm and the shrill cries of men—as a clock which has stopped ticking off the time is aloof from the currents of noisy life which flow past it.

"Apparently the crew had gone wild, and the captain, too, had completely lost his head, for we passed him sobbing on the deck, unable to give us a coherent word. The men were fighting like freshmen in a college rush over lifeboats which they were attempting to lower to the water.

" 'No chance here,' growled Lutz. 'Lord, let's get out of this mess!'

"I trailed him forward, battling against the wind and the waves which broke over the deck. Once I stumbled over a big brute who was on his knees blubbering like a child. I shook him: "What did we hit?'

" 'Reef. She's a-goin' down, sir—a goin' down. May the good, kind Lord have mercy—'

"Another time I might have pitied this snivelling creature who could not die like a man, but now I stepped over him, intent upon keeping an eye upon Lutz, even as he was intent upon keeping an eye upon me. Lutz was far forward, clinging to a rail, staring over the ship's side. I reached him, clung with him, and followed his gaze.

"There below us, close against the ship, bobbled a little white dory, looking as frail as an eggshell upon the dim, surging mass of waters; it had been launched probably in the first wild moment, and then abandoned for the heavier, more seaworthy boats.

" 'A chance,' spoke Lutz. 'I'll—risk it!'

"He turned to me then, and his eye rested speculatively upon the pocket of my coat which held the vase.

" 'No, you don't!' I said sharply. 'I'll take that risk with you.'

"We stood measuring each other. It was a contest of wills that threatened any moment to degenerate into a physical struggle. 'Oh, I see you are thinking it unlikely'—Twining's long-fingered, nervous old hand shaded his eyes from the candlelight—'that we two men should have stood there wrestling over a Greek vase when any moment threatened to plunge us into eternity. But if you cannot believe that, young man, then you know nothing of the collector's passion or the scholar's passion.

"We measured each other, I say—oh, quietly. All about us was the terror of the storm—the same wash and slap and snarl that you hear now about this very house; and concentrating upon him, probing him, my heart filled with intense hatred of him, slowly and surely, as a jug that is held under a single stream fills with water—such a hatred as threatened to overflow—a *killing* hatred! There, on just such a night as this, murder was born in me—murder, I tell you!

"The crisis passed. Unexpectedly, Lutz gave in: 'Oh, all right; together still—for a little time—'

"A wave drenched us. We recovered, strained into the darkness to determine whether the little dory had been swamped. But no, she still rode the sea, miraculously right side up.

" 'Come along, then!' snapped Lutz. 'There's no time to waste.'

"Our time was indeed short. We gathered what store of things we could together, and since the decks of the ship were by this time ominously close to the water, the drop into the tossing small dory was easier than it might have been. Lutz took the oars. Some way he had maneuvered us about the bow of the ship, and now we were clear of the sinking vessel, carried swiftly away from it by the sea.

"The rest is a blur. I recall dark shapes—bits of bobbing wreckage—and the white circle of an empty life saver. I did not see the ship go down. One minute there were lights; and the next minute there was darkness over all the ocean, and the human voices had subsided into the voices of wind and water. For the sea itself claimed all my attention and held it.

"That night was a business of separate, marching waves, with a separate prayer for each wave, that it would not break at the wrong moment. A hundred times I shut my eyes and abandoned hope, and a hundred times I opened them and found us safe. Lutz, an athlete in his day, hung onto the oars, but he was powerless against that surge of water. It was only a miracle which kept us afloat. Our little dory rode the waves like a cork, but she still rode them.

"With the breaking of the sullen dawn, the wind died. The rain settled to a steady downpour, and the waves, as the day wore on, subsided to the long, low rollers that last for hours after such a gale. The gray sea was a vast, unbroken stretch without a trace of life; perhaps the miracle that had saved our frail boat had not held for those heavier dories . . .

"Anyway, to cut it short, we drifted that day without sight of a single vessel. Wet through and numb with cold, I was glad to take a shift at the oars while Lutz slept. Our hastily gathered provisions were found to consist of half a pail of soda biscuits, a lantern without oil, some miscellaneous ropes and tarpaulins—and that was all!

"We ate sparingly of the biscuits, drank rain water caught in the cracker pail. Our boat, we discovered, was leaking badly through seams in the bow; so we crowded as much weight to the stern of the craft as we could, and I was kept busy bailing out the water.

"Late in the afternoon, when the situation looked worst, we perceived a black speck upon the horizon. The speck grew into a pile of dark rocks—bare and uninhabited, we saw, as the current carried us close. Somehow, we gained the sheltered side of the island, and there, in a narrow inlet, achieved a landing. The mass of rocks was perhaps fourteen hundred feet long and half as wide. It rose abruptly from the sea, a lonely, desolate pile. The only life was sea gulls, insects and spiders, and a few fish in the surrounding waters. We were together there on the island for four days.

"Through all those four days, half starved and suffering from exposure as we were, Lutz and I nursed each his own half of the cylix and kept a watchful eye upon the other half. The strain of the situation grew intolerable. Now through what follows I don't know how to account for myself; whether it was a fever working in my blood—but no, I was coldly, calculatingly sane as I laid my plans. Yet before that crisis I had never in my life been a vicious man.

"You see, figuring our location from the ship's map as near as I could remember it, I came to believe that this solitary rock was one visited and described by Darwin in his investigation of volcanic islands. If it was the island I believed it to be, then it lay off the ocean lines and was very rarely passed by ships. Our chance of being rescued, if we stayed on the island then, was slight.

"I did not mention these deductions to Lutz. Nor, after Lutz had eaten our last cracker, did I tell him of my own small reserve supply of concentrated meat, which I carried always in my pocket at that time to save the trouble of too frequent meals. At first I did not myself comprehend the drift of my own thoughts.

"Then, on the second night, while Lutz slept under a tarpaulin and while I fought off a twisting hunger, I saw the event quite clearly. Lutz would be the first to succumb to weakness; I would hold on longer than he could. The boat was our best risk, but in its present leaky condition it was unseaworthy for two men. Now *one man*, huddled back in the stern . . . there was just a chance. And the vase—the *whole* vase—in my possession; and my article secure . .
.

"Deliberately, I broke off a piece of the dried meat, which I had not touched until that moment.

"Perhaps I should have weakened in my course and divided my slender provision with him—I do not know. But on the following morning Lutz, sprawled on his stomach over the rock's edge, with his pocketknife tied to a pole, managed to spear a small fish. He did not share with me. Desperate for food, he devoured the thing raw, and the sight nauseated and hardened me.

"I begrudged him the strength he was storing up; but I did not doubt the issue. For all his athletic build, Lutz was soft with soft living. Moreover, my will was stronger than his. So I ate sparingly of my dried meat while Lutz slept, and I maintained a patient watch over the Euphronios fragment which was not yet in my hands.

"Meantime, I kept up some pretense of friendship and good cheer with him. He insisted upon piling up wet driftwood for a fire in case a ship should come our way, and I encouraged him to the effort; though we had no matches, he thought he might manage a spark, and while I knew that this rock was too soft to serve as flint, I agreed with him.

"I watched him burn up energy and grow hourly weaker, and waited . . . waited . . .

V

"Murder was in the air between us, and since those things breed, I wondered that a murdering hatred of me did not spring up in his heart to match my own, and that he did not tackle me there on the rocks and fight it out with me.

"But no—though I sometimes fancied he looked at me oddly, he remained amiable. Lutz was as determined as I to have his way about the vase; beyond that, he was still my friend in his loose, selfish way—my friend as much as he had ever been. As my friend, Lutz, gross and unscrupulous as he was, could never have guessed the thing that was going on in my mind. That was my great sin, the crime that makes me doubly cursed; it was my friend whom I betrayed—a man who was bound to me in friendship.

"When, on the fourth day, the rain ceased, and a hot, tropical sun blazed out and dried up the pools in the rocks which had furnished our water, I felt myself slipping. The heat on those naked rocks was worse than the chilling rain. A fever grew in me. I could not afford to wait longer. While my companion drowsed in a kind of stupor, I gathered a few things into the boat, stowed my own precious fragment in a concealed nook far up in the bow, and then moved cautiously toward Lutz.

"A dizziness seized me . . . but I went on . . . I had rehearsed it all fifty times, you understand, so that I knew every move by heart; and though my memory of the actual events is not clear, I must have gone through with it as I had planned. I suppose I may have awakened him in shoving off the boat, for I have a hazy recollection of a fight.

"And when I came to, alone in the dory, in a calm blue sea, I felt a soreness at my throat, and afterward I was to find black finger marks there, which I carried with me for days. Perhaps I had actually killed him, left him in a heap on the rocks—I couldn't remember. But whether I had murdered him outright with my own hands or not, it did not matter; I had murdered him as surely by abandoning him there on that forgotten island and taking the one chance for myself. I was a murderer by intent and by cold calculation—a murderer of my friend and colleague!"

"And your own fate?" I prompted old "Tinker" Twining gently.

"I was picked up several days later, in a state of semi-consciousness, by a small passenger steamer, just as I had foreseen. In the long voyage home, I lived through nightmares. I felt impelled to confess the truth and to beg the Captain to turn back for Lutz, but I knew that it was now too late. I suffered alone as I deserved to suffer.

"There were nights when I felt my fingers sinking into the flesh of his throat . . . other nights when I looked at my own hands and could not believe it. My half of the vase—did I tell you that I must somehow have failed to secure Lutz's half, strong as my determination had been, since only this fragment was found in the dory, hidden under the bow where I had placed it? This piece, though I hated it in my reaction, I kept always before me as the reminder, the sackcloth and ashes of my sin.

"The steamer landed me in Boston, and I wandered up here to the Cape. Since the *Agricola* had gone down with all souls reported lost, I was dead to the world. That was well, for, having murdered my friend for a piece of pottery, I was unfit for human society. This penalty of my crime followed as a natural sequence: to drop out of the world and the work I loved; to read no books and to take no periodicals on my own subject; in short, to give up the thing that was most vital to me. That would be prison for me—a prison worse than most criminals ever know.

"I found this remote house, got in touch with my lawyer at home, and, having pledged him to secrecy, arranged that my small, yearly income should be paid regularly to a T. Twining at this address. I had no close relatives, and the old lawyer has long since died, leaving my affairs in the hands of an incurious younger partner. There was no hitch.

"So I settled here, and eked out my income with this painting. Though I fixed my own terms of imprisonment, I have lived up to them. In all those forty years I have permitted myself no inquiries and I have heard no news of anyone I ever knew in the old days. I have virtually buried myself alive.

"Ah, you are thinking it wrong of me to have buried, too, the half of this valuable cylix, since, fragment though it is, it would have been sufficient to establish the fact. Perhaps it *was* wrong. But, don't you see, I could establish nothing without first revealing my identity and giving my word as a scientist that the shard came from the Persian debris? That way lay danger—the danger of being drawn back into the old life; there, too, lay honor for me who deserved nothing but contempt.

"And always in the background there was Lorna Story. No, the temptations were too many; I could not risk it. But I have bequeathed that knowledge to posterity; I have left a written confession and a statement. Tell me—you have recently come out of the world—you don't think it will be too late after my death, do you?"

Though I had some shadowy idea of what extensive excavations and what far-reaching discoveries had been made in the classical world of recent years, I assured the old man that it would perhaps not be too late. I had not the heart to rob him of the little outworn theory that he hugged close.

"And so," he concluded his story, "you see before you a murderer! Your verdict would be—?"

"But how can you be sure?" I countered. "If you slipped up on the vase, you may have slipped up on other details of your program. Besides, his chance on the island was as good as yours in a leaking dory. Who shall say?"

Old Twining merely shook his head. He returned again to the glowing fragment on the table between us.

"Ah, you are thinking that the vase is my consolation—that I wanted to keep it. And perhaps I did," he owned wistfully. "I swear to you I abhor the deed it stands for, but I can no more help loving it in itself —" He lost himself, wandered off once more into the fine points of his treasure.

But the wind rose up again, and the old man's head dropped to his hands. I was with him all that night and I saw him suffer the tortures of an eternally damned soul with a razor blade conscience.

The storm over, he was the kindly, considerate host when he bade goodbye on the following morning. I left him with the feeling that I had been in the presence of as fine a gentleman as I had ever met; that his story of the preceding night was utterly incongruous to the man as he was. It would be a physical impossibility, I protested, for that gentle old scholar to harm an insect.

His mind had wandered at times: could it be that he was suffering some kind of an hallucination, the result, perhaps, of an overacute conscience? I believed there was some factor to his story which I had not got hold of, and I promised myself to visit him again.

VI

But time passed. I was abroad in England and in France. Then two years later, back again in New York, I picked up the missing link in the old scholar's story:

It was inevitable, I suppose, that, as buyer for the House of Harrow, I should sooner or later stumble into Max Bauer. At a private sale I lazily bid against the wealthy collector for a jade bowl and good-naturedly lost to him. I talked with him, and when he urged me to dine with him that evening and see his treasures, I assented.

I don't know why I accepted his invitation, for I did not like the man; but I was mildly curious about his collection, and alone in the city in midsummer, I welcomed any diversion.

So he dined me and wined me—especially the latter—to repleteness in the ornate dining-room of his luxurious apartment, which was after the manner of a banquet hall. I watched him pick apart the bird that was set before him, and found something cannibalistic in the performance; and I watched him again over a rich mousse, and liked him less and less. His hand was always upon the bottle; he gave me no peace—urged things upon me, made a show of his food and his service.

The meal over, still keeping the decanter by him, he trailed me through rooms littered with oriental junk. He bragged and boasted, told the history of this piece and that: how he had robbed one man here and tricked another there. His voice thickened, as his enthusiasm grew, and I turned thoroughly uncomfortable and wondered when I could break away.

Clearly, the man attracted few friends of a caliber to appreciate his art treasures, for under my perfunctory approval, he became increasingly garrulous, until at last he invited me into the inner shrine, the small room which held his most private and precious possessions.

We stopped before a water color painting of a slim girl in gray. "My wife," said old Bauer with a flourish. "Her last portrait."

I turned incredulously from that white-flower face, with its fine, subtle smile, half-ironical and half-tired, to my gross-featured host—and I shuddered.

"A handsome woman," he mumbled. "Picture doesn't do her justice. Face so-so, but a body . . . a body for an artist to paint . . ."

I looked away from him—followed the gray girl's eyes to the object below her upon which she ironically smiled: it was a red-figured Greek vase, and I remember thinking that this man must have changed—that his taste, his very life, must have degenerated, like the retrogression from the fine to the decadent, since such a girl had married him.

Then something familiar in the vase struck me—like the broken pattern of a forgotten dream . . . It was the fragment of a vase, the half of a cylix, on which an orange goddess stood with uplifted spear.

"Ah," I breathed, "the Athena—Euphronios!"

"So you're up to it!" chuckled old Bauer. "Not many of 'em are. Classic stuff: I used to aim for a collection of the pure Greek, but I've grown out of that; not that I wouldn't have achieved it if my taste hadn't changed, y'understand, for I'm generally successful—I get the things I set out for.

This —" he scowled at the vase—"is my one failure. But there's a story,"—he poured himself another whisky (to my infinite relief forgot to press me)—"want to hear it, eh?"

I looked at him carefully: the plump fingers; the full, sensual lips; the dark skin and the nose—probably Jewish blood. What was the name?—Lutz, that was it!

Decidedly, I did want to hear his story!

VII

"My one failure," he emphasized it, slumping into a chair. "Not my fault, either; the fault of a stuffy old fool. He doted on me, played the fatherly role and I tolerated him as you will such folks. I cribbed a lot off of him; I was keen on the classics at that time, and he knew a thing or two.

"Besides, he was sweet on Lorna, and you never could tell about her—odd tastes; it was best to keep track of him. We traveled together for the college—you'd never guess I'd been a college professor in my day, would you? I happened onto this thing quite by luck—a genuine Euphronios, broken clean in two pieces. I wanted it, and I managed it. This fellow—old Gooding—had a notion of turning it in to the college museum; he had some other fool's idea of proving something-or-other—a rare, old bird, a pedant, you understand. It was a shaky business; I'd no intention of publishing my Euphronios at this time. But he was set—you'd never believe how set!—and since I couldn't afford to stir up a row there in Athens, I humored him.

"Once we were clear of Greece—once we struck home ground—but we never struck home ground on that ship. She went down!"—with a flourish of his glass. "Yes, dammit all, regular desert island stuff. We were hung up on a rock in mid-ocean, the two of us, old Gooding hugging tight to half the vase, and me nursing the other half. Can't say I ever was more damned uncomfortable in my life.

"He had this eccentric idea of honor and he had it hard like religion, and he hung on like a bulldog. It was war between us. Oh, he doted upon me right enough, still insisted upon the paternal role, but I'd no intention of letting him pull this thing."

Again Bauer fumbled for the bottle, spilled whisky into his glass.

"The old idiot—you'd think he'd've seen what he was driving me to, but not him. I had a couple of matches in my pocket—I'd held out on him, y'understand. And I'd built up a pile of driftwood for a signal fire to the first ship that passed. But I'd no notion of saving *him*, too. No, I had a contrary notion of setting him adrift in the dory.

"Oh, it was easy: he'd gone weaker than a cat, y'understand—all gray matter an' no physh—physhique, ol' Cheever Gooding. I'd take my chances on the island with a heap of dry wood an' two matches for a l'il bonfire, an' with the c-cup, both pieces of it safe.

"*Murder?*" Bauer laughed. "'s'n ugly word, eh?" He pursued with an uncertain finger an injured fly which crawled across his trousers leg. "Bah, they say this man kills for hate, that for love—all good, noble motives. But your true collector—you 'n' me—kills for a c-cup. Killing's natural—th'easiest thing in the world—when you're preshed for time. 'N I was preshed for time, see? There was a ship out there—I saw the smoke. I got him into the dory, but it was a fight; there was life in the ol' bird yet, though the sun'd laid him low. Leaky boat—not much chance for him—still I'd be sure. I choked him gently—oh, quite gently—like thish,"—Bauer demonstrated by crushing the fly very thoroughly between his thumb and

forefinger—"till the breath was gone from him. Then I looked for
th'other half of the vashe—couldn't find it. The smoke was
close—couldn't wait. P'raps he's hid it in the rocks, I shay. So I
shoves him off, an' the tide carries him 'way from the ship's
smoke—bob-bobbin' away.

"I runs up an' sends my twigs a-blazin' to the sky. 'N I searches
everywhere for the c-cup—in every crack—an' no luck! Guns
shalute—ship's comin'; li'l dory bobs off there a mere sun spot; still
no luck. Can you beat it? All my work for nothing! 'Cause, see, I'd
murdered him—an' what for? Damn him, his skin's too cheap —

"Say, you're not leavin'? My one failure—I've had everything
else: Lorna an' thish here c-c'lection—everything! But this one l'il
broken c-cup—too bad—too bad —"

I left him caressing the vase with his hands as old "Tinker"
Twining had caressed it with his eyes. But before I went, my gaze
fell again upon the painting of Bauer's wife, and I remembered the
other man's words for her: "A beautiful mind, and a light shining
through her gray eyes that was like the haunting line of a poem."

"Body love and soul love," I muttered.

Bauer sought me out the following morning.

"What did I tell you last night?" he asked.

I told him briefly.

"Fiction!" he shrugged with an uneasy laugh. "I get to running
on—You'll forget it?"

I was ready for him.

"Yes," I agreed. "I'll forget it—on one condition: that you run
down to the Cape with me to—pass judgment on an antique; to give
me your honest, expert advice—free of charge."

He consented at once, the connoisseur in him aroused.

VIII

So we came down to the Cape on a clear blue morning after rains.

I made inquiries at the village concerning old "Tinker" Twining,
and was prepared for what I found. I had come in time, a woman told
me; she was troubled about him, though, since he would allow no
one to stop in the house and care for him.

We took the trail over to the back shore; and I held Bauer off,
answered his questions vaguely. It was a different day from that

sullen one on which I had first walked this path; an exquisite morning, requiring you to capture the shine of each separate leaf—the upward-tossed, silver poplar leaves and the varnished oak leaves—if you would adequately describe it.

This meeting I had planned solely for the sake of the old scholar; if, in aiding Twining to clear his conscience, I also cleared the conscience of Max Bauer, that I could not help. But Bauer, I assured myself, had no conscience; one way or the other, it would not matter to him.

Still, it was a situation without parallel, I thought: two men, each living, and each believing himself to have murdered the other. And to bring those two men together, face to face, would be smashing drama!

But life is seldom as spectacular as we anticipate; my fireworks fizzled. Beyond a stretch of beach grass—running silver under the sunlight—and humped up there precariously over sands, stood the same little rusty gray house. The door was half open, and the work bench was deserted. We found the old man in a bedroom over the sea, lying in a black walnut bed under a patchwork quilt.

He was propped up on pillows, and the worn face was silhouetted against the ocean, blue today with pale sweepings, and flowing out to silver under the sun. The elderly scholar was delirious, his mind wandering over that old sin; he was still paying the penalty for a murder of the imagination.

"My friend," he muttered, "the man who was bound to me in friendship—certain death —"

"Listen!" I said. "This is Max Bauer, the man you thought you killed! You didn't murder him; you only *thought* you did. He's here safe—look!"

But the other did not grasp it; only repeated the name "Max Bauer," and turned away with a long shudder.

Then Bauer was chattering at my shoulder: "*Gooding*—old Cheever Gooding himself!"

"Perhaps that's what *you* called him—the man you strangled—It's no use—no earthly use; he's still under the illusion — we can never make it clear to him now."

"But how—?" I turned impatiently at Bauer's insistence, gave him curtly and succinctly, in four sentences, the clues he had missed.

He sat there. "So he tried to murder me! The old—skunk!"

And later, "B'God," he whispered, "how he's gone! A shadow..."

I looked at Bauer, sitting corpulent and gross.

"Yes," I replied, "a shadow."

But already Bauer's eyes had roved from Twining to a thing on the quilt which he had missed in the patchwork colors, a thing of orange and black.

"Lord, it's the missing half!" he exclaimed, and now there was genuine feeling in his voice.

I stood between Bauer and that object, guarding Twining's treasure. And still I tried to give old Twining back his clear conscience.

"It's Max Bauer," I insinuated, "Max Bauer."

I must have got it across for as Bauer edged closer and as I seized the shard, the old man stared at that sensual, dark face with an expression of recognition. There must have come to him then some inkling of the situation.

"Yes," he whispered, "let him have it." He took the fragment from me, held it up tenderly for a moment in his two frail, fine old hands, and then placed it in the thick hands of Max Bauer. Bauer closed upon it greedily.

"Murdered him!" moaned Twining.

"Murdered me nothing," chuckled Bauer, who could now, with the vase in his grasp, afford to be generous. "'S all right, old man; we're quits."

But Twining was fumbling for a piece of paper. "This!" he breathed. "Tell them where—painting before sculpture —"

"But great Caesar, they've known all this for forty years!" exploded Bauer, scanning the written statement. "Why, they've found fragments of another Euphronios in that same Persian dirt heap; someone else proved that very thing and the Lord knows how many other things. Just fragments though, y'understand—not a perfect one like this." Bauer let the paper flutter from his hands; I quietly picked up Twining's confession and later dropped it into the stove. The old man relapsed into his former state of wandering misery, with apparently no recollection of the episode.

Bauer left soon after that.

"A good day for me, and I owe it all to you, Van Nuys—My thanks," he made genial acknowledgment from the doorway.

I choked on my disgust of him. So Max Bauer, whom only circumstances outside of himself had saved from actual murder, went up to the city, successful and carefree, to add to his many treasures old "Tinker" Twining's one treasure.

I stayed with the old scholar, whose every instinct would have held him from the murder he had planned, and watched him wear himself out, suffering to the last breath for his one mental sin.

That is why I hope at the final reckoning, God will take some account of the sensitiveness of the souls he weighs, and will fix his penalties accordingly.

SEPTEMBER 1923

Volume II, Number 2 is marginally better than its predecessor, thanks in part to Otis Adelbert Kline's atmospheric "The Cup of Blood," which collectors generally consider to be the best of Kline's early contributions to *Weird Tales*. Sixth of the thirteen issues that Edwin Baird would edit, September 1923 contains an article on black magic, Preston Langley Hickey's third "The Cauldron" feature, and sixteen stories, including a reprint of Ambrose Bierce's tired old warhorse, "The Damned Thing," and lesser efforts by Julian Kilman, Vincent Starrett and Farnsworth Wright. One of the two serial installments is the first half of "The People of the Comet" by Austin Hall, coauthor with Homer Eon Flint of "The Blind Spot," an indifferently-written but popular and conceptually striking science-fantasy novel that first appeared in 1921 in "Argosy Magazine." In addition to Kline's story, I have chosen James Ravenscroft's nasty period piece about vivisection, "The Bloodstained Parasol," and the obscure and possibly pseudonymous P. D. Gog's grim Hawaiian anecdote, "The Dead-Naming of Lukapehu." The latter has a ring of authenticity and might well be a true story.

The Dead-Naming of Lukapehu

By P. D. GOG

The following tale was handed to me in manuscript by an acquaintance to whom it was related by a friend who heard it from an old resident of the Hawaiian group as happening to his father. In view of the father's integrity, and bearing in mind other similar cases, there is, of course, no doubt as to the truth of the story. Whether Lukapehu died of an "error of mortal judgement," of the incantations of the old medicine man, or of superstitious fear, is for the reader to judge for himself.

The title Kahuna means sorcerer. Kahuna-anana is a specific title for a death-dealing sorcerer, from a Kahuna a sorcerer; and anana, to gaze intently. The epithet suggests that ancient belief in the evil eye, so naively preserved in the Scottish ballads, and particularly common in Italy and India. The story is recorded here substantially as it came into my possession.

In 1859, my father had already established himself on a large plantation of Kawai, one of the Hawaiian group. He acquired among his "boys" a reputation for utter fearlessness and, to an astonishing degree, for foolhardy disregard of the various powers of enchantment. There dwelt also on Kawai, where the two branches of the Waimea River join, a famous old Kahuna, Kapukapu, who far surpassed his fellow sorcerers in skill, being reputed a Kahuna-anana or death-dealing sorcerer. So great was the reputation of this magician that never did any of the villagers presume to oppose his wishes; but often they complained bitterly to my father of Kapukapu's unjust demands for food and service, exacted under threats of fearful and certain calamity. My father pooh-poohed these tales, particularly to a certain one of his boys, Lukapehu, his most skillful fisherman, exhorting him to have no fear of the old man but to face him boldly and laugh his threats to scorn.

One evening in the year I have mentioned, Lukapehu came up the valley as the sun was setting, carrying in his net the day's catch, which had been large even for him. He was a tall, good-natured native, swinging along with the care-free abandon of superfluous physical strength and primitive irresponsibility. Perhaps his savage heart was touched by the glory of the sunset, which was reflected from the palms and tropic ferns in a golden aura; perhaps he was thinking of the wife and the naked little bambino who would greet him at his hut and rejoice with him in the silver treasure his skill has wrested from the sea; for as he strode up the deep valley of the Waimea River, he sang a plaintive melody that mingled with the twilight like the lengthening shadows, faint, elusive.

Suddenly the song ceased and an uncanny silence pervaded the ravine, save for the swish of the river and the twitter of the restless birds in the koa trees. Lukapehu had reached the branching tributaries where Kapukapu dwelt. Silhouetted against the fiery sun, stood the old sorcerer, tall, gaunt, leaning upon his staff and gazing intently down the valley. Clöthed only in a ragged loin cloth, his long, unkempt hair brushing his shoulders, his thin, gray beard stirring in the evening breeze, his eyes bulging like fire brands from his cadaverous skull, he looked like the animated skeleton of a fiend. When he saw the fisherman with his burden, he crossed the stream and stopped Lukapehu.

"My son," he said, "I see how great has been your success. When a young man has so much it is well for him to share with an old man."

Lukapehu, fortified by my father's example, replied boldly, "It is well also, sometimes, for an old man to mind his own business."

Brushing past the gaunt Kapukapu, he continued up the valley, ignoring the calling of his name by the enraged sorcerer. But presently he heard the Kahuna chanting over strange, sonorous syllables which gathered intensity and resonance as the voice went on, until from the low, menacing hum of vowels, the Kahuna had raised the echoes of the valley and the wood with his reverberant chant, "Lukapehu shall die!"

Lukapehu's heart sank. He tried to reassure himself with the recollection of my father's words, but primitive fear was fast laying hold on his soul. How could civilization free from bondage in a single generation, a life which was the product of ages of superstitious slavery! Had not the evil Kahuna-anana called the fatal curse down upon his cousin, and had he not perished miserably? How could he, Lukapehu, hope to escape??

He looked back . . . and was lost! The sun had gone down leaving a bloody reflection in a cloud-bespattered sky; the shadows lay black and threatening among the palms. Beside the darkly mumbling stream stood Kapukapu, his ragged hair fluttering in the quickening breeze, his long arms extended toward the terrified Lukapehu, while he muttered his diabolical dead-naming, "Lukapehu shall die! Lukapehu shall die!"

The poor fisherman sank exhausted before the door of his hut saying over and over, "I am dying; Kapukapu has called me! I am dying! I am dying!

His frightened wahine and the little brown bambino dragged him into the house and sent for my father. But he was busy and sent word back that Lukapehu should not fear, he could not die, and that he, my father, would come down in the morning.

The next morning, just before dawn, while the dew was still heavy on the ferns and the pandanus, he rode over to the hut of the fisherman expecting to find him about his work. But Lukapehu still lay moaning on his cot, nor could my father raise him up.

He died with the breaking of the day, just as the sun dispelled the gloom of the Waimea valley, called to his death by the hideous Kahuna-anana.

The Bloodstained Parasol:
A Study in Madness

JAMES RAVENSCROFT

Within the room were sounds that were unpleasant to hear. They were dreadful maniacal shouts of command, shrill cries of terror, the more awful because constantly broken by hoarseness, and moanings of infinite tenderness and sadness.

"He is in one of his spells," the attendant said. "Perhaps it would be just as well not to see him now. It is not a picture that you would want to carry with you."

The attendant's voice was one of gentle solicitude and pathos. Doubtless long service in the place had made it so. It was a private sanitarium in the National Capital, for the hopelessly insane, to which my profession as specialist and alienist gained me admittance.

The sounds hypnotized me: I could not turn away. The small iron grating in the upper part of the door drew me like a magnet, and I went and looked into the room.

A pale-faced, emaciated, wild-looking man, standing in the middle of a bare mattress on a heavy iron bedstand, was yelling and gesticulating madly at some imaginary object at the bottom of the door.

"Get away, curse you, get away!" he cried frantically. "Begone, you brute! Out of my sight! Would to God I had burned you as fine as ashes! Oh-h-h-h-h! Oh-h-h-h-h!"

The groans which ended the fury cannot be described; they were those of a soul in agony. His whole appearance was that of one convulsed with a terror as of death.

At first he did not see me as I peered through the grating; his eyes bright with the glitter of madness, were fixed in a fearful stare at the bottom of the door.

"It is over for a while," said the attendant.

The words roused the man and he raised his eyes to the grating. A wan smile of relief broke the expression of horror on his face, and he at once stepped off the bed and came to the door. A beady sweat, not the kind caused by heat, though the day was sultry, was on his brow and upper lip, and his body relaxing from the tension of the spell, was shaking with a nervous palsy. He was clad in pajamas of some coarse white material and his feet were bare.

"Pardon me," he spoke in low tones and with an accent of breeding, "but that infernal dog distracted my attention and I didn't see you. I'm glad you came. I remember you quite well, indeed. You were doing interne work, were you not?" I yielded to his humor, grateful that I could help to ease his tortured spirit, and nodded affirmatively.

The glitter in his eyes seemed to be intensified, and putting his face almost against the grating, as though he meant his speech to be confidential, he said:

"Perhaps you saw her?" His voice was almost a whisper. "She came in when I was dissecting. I was always dissecting then, always dissecting. Understand? I cut things up, alive and dead, dead and alive. That was the beginning of the hell."

He said it so sanely, so remorsefully that I, startled, looked closely at him. Reason appeared to be reinstated on her throne. Then he broke out again.

"I cut them to pieces, but I didn't burn the pieces and they escaped, out of the windows, through the keyhole. They even hid in the pockets of my clothes until I was on the street, and then they would leap out and dart away."

He moistened his thin, dry lips with his tongue and took hold of the bars of the grating and went on:

"No, I didn't burn the pieces and they escaped. That dog follows me in pieces. At night its feet scratch the bottom of the door and its eyes look in between the bars of this window. Its red, dripping tongue lies on the bed beside me and its hot, horrible breath smothers me. Its footsteps trot up and down the floor and its hellish moans and whines drive me crazy. Listen! It was alive. That's why she struck me! A soft, white thing it was, and I threw up my hand and caught it. She dropped it and I took it and kept it. That's it, standing in the corner over there."

Involuntarily I shuddered and looked toward the corner designated by his gesture. There was nothing in any of the corners.

"And after the dog is gone, she comes. She comes, slipping, slipping. I can't hear her, I can't see her. She comes to get her parasol. But when she sees the bloodstains on it she turns to a ghost. I try to wash the stains out, but I can't. Every time I put water on them, they spread."

He leaned closer to the bars, and with one eye cautiously on the attendant, he whispered:

"I'm working on a solution that will entirely remove the bloodstains, so she will take the parasol, for when she does the dog will leave, and then I can get a long, quiet rest."

He paused and looked furtively around the room, and then began his awful babblings again.

He called piteously after me as the attendant took my arm and drew me away. I remembered little else that I saw in the sanitarium. "Tell me about him," I implored, as soon as we were out of hearing of his cries. "Who is he? How did he come to be here?"

The attendant hesitated.

"Not every one should hear that story," he remarked, thoughtfully, as if half talking to himself, "but, of course, with you, a specialist, it is different."

He took me to a chair on a porch. From there I could see into a section of the grounds of the inmates, where benighted beings were engaging in assuming their various and fantastic roles of madness.

"His name I shall not tell you," he began, "for that is a secret and very properly so. I shall only relate briefly what happened to him, as it came to me from his mother. His people are prominent and wealthy. It wrecked his mother's life, but the only thing that could be done was to give him up to this place. When they come here to see him they wait until he is comparatively free from symptoms of an attack, and then they go look in at the grating, as you did. Strange to tell, he recognizes only one of them, a sister, but he believes her to be a sister who died some two or three years before he became insane.

"Every possible care is given him and every famous specialist in the country has examined him. They say it is useless to hope; that he will be raving mad to the end of his days. When the fury seizes him he will hurl at his imaginary tormentors anything he can lift. That is why his room has nothing in it but a bed, and that is fastened to the floor with heavy cleats. The mattress, made of material that resists his nails, is securely attached to steel slats riveted to the bed frame, and there is no covering. Blankets, spreads, pillows and sheets were given him at first and he rent them to tatters fighting the 'dog'. In the winter his room is kept so warm that covering is not needed.

"His was accounted one of the brightest minds at the medical college in which he was a professor. It was predicted that he would do great things in surgery. He was making a special research in the field of vivisection. As he himself says, every time he can get some one to listen, that was the beginning of the hell.

"He was engaged to marry one of the loveliest young women of his city. From what I was told, she was as lovely in spirit as she was in person. The woman, it was said, was the real force that moved his work at such amazing strides. He was eager to give her of the very best of his energies and talents.

"As a quiet and close observer of life, I am sometimes almost persuaded to believe in fate. The story is that a whim possessed his fiancee to 'go through' the medical college, just, I presume, as a whim possessed you to go through this place. She said nothing to him of her intention for she wanted to surprise him.

"Two girl friends accompanied her, and together they explored. An attendant, who must have been exceedingly careless, was directing them, and at a certain place in their adventure fate willed that he should be called elsewhere for a few minutes. In those few minutes a man was doomed to madness, a woman's heart was broken, and several lives were made desolate.

"The place where the attendant left them was a corridor by the laboratory where dissecting and other experimental work was done. The doctor's fiancee opened the door of the room and peeped in. At the opposite side a man with his back to her was working over some object. She at once recognized the familiar figure, and, as fate would have it, she was seized with the caprice to steal up behind him. Telling her companions who he was, and bidding them wait in the corridor for the attendant, she went in, softly closed the door and noiselessly tiptoed along the aisle between benches.

"If there had been more light—but why say 'if,' other than if fate had not taken her there that day? Her lightly-slippered feet made no sound and she stood behind him unnoticed. He might have heard, but he was deeply engrossed in his work.

"She tilted slightly on one foot to look past him at the object which so held his attention. She gazed a moment, and then, as though forgetting his presence, she sprang to his side. A dog was stretched on the dissecting board. How she discovered the fact is a mystery, unless she saw with the inner and more penetrating vision, but she did see evidences of life in an animal that had been carefully prepared, by all the modern methods, as a subject for the dissector. "The doctor dropped his instrument and stood staring at her, speechless. Had she dropped from above he could not have been more amazed and startled.

" 'It is alive!' the girl gasped.

" 'Yes,' he admitted. 'You had better not look at it. Please come away. How did you get here?'

"The girl never moved nor took her eyes from him.

" 'It is in the interest of science of saving and preserving human life.' he began to explain. No doubt a cold fear was creeping into his heart at the sight of her. 'It is done in nearly all colleges and hospitals, you know. The animal is under a powerful anesthetic and does not feel pain.'

"A moment more she stood, so the tale goes, as though transfixed, and then—

" 'You fiend, you coward!' she screamed, as she struck him in the face with her parasol. She swung it with all her strength for a second blow and he threw up his hands to ward it off. There were red smears where he touched it, and when she saw them she flung the parasol from her and swooned.

"Her companions, from where they were waiting in the corridor, heard the scream and the commotion, and rushed in just as the doctor was picking her up, and ran after him as he carried her to another room. He told them that she had fainted at the sight of the dissecting table.

"It was a fatal day for the doctor. In his excitement he had forgotten to wipe his hands before he lifted the girl, and there were red finger marks on her white dress. Almost as soon as she revived she saw them, and swooned again. And when she again revived she began trying to tear off the dress, like she had lost her reason. One of her companions telephoned to her home and fresh clothes were brought. It was perhaps all of an hour later when, sick and too weak to walk, she was carried from the room to which the doctor had taken her.

"That was the end. The doctor pleaded with the girl's father and mother, but in vain. She never again permitted him to see her. She said she would as soon marry a murdered. Night after night he paced the sidewalk in front of her home, and went away only when the lateness of the hour and the vacancy of the street made him conspicuous.

"He gave up his college work, neglected his personal appearance, and at last became like a haunted man. Many dark tales of what happened were whispered among friends and acquaintances of the two families. The girl became a nervous wreck and finally her people broke up their home and moved to a distant city.

"Then something in the doctor's brain cracked, and, well—you have seen for yourself."

He rose, a gentle reminder that he could not then spare me more of his time. As we shook hands in parting, he said:

"Vivisection may, possibly, be of service to medical and surgical science, but it has nothing to do with love."

OCTOBER 1923

October was 1923's most vital issue because Bob Weinberg explains in *The Weird Tales Story*, "It featured the first appearance of three authors all who were to become top names in the fantastic fiction field"—H. P. Lovecraft, Frank Owen and Seabury Quinn.

Second only to Farnsworth Wright's influence, Lovecraft's work and ongoing networking with other writers had the greatest impact on the contents of *Weird Tales* for years to come. His first story, "Dagon," though neither his best nor worst, deserves inclusion for its historical significance.

Unfortunately, the same cannot be said of Seabury Quinn's debut. With a total of fourteen articles and 146 stories, Quinn is *Weird Tales*'s most prolific author and his work is often first-rate. But "The Phantom Farmhouse," though often reprinted, is an unconvincing lycanthropic yarn with a spectacularly dense protagonist. Better, though beyond the scope of this collection, is Quinn's article, "Weird Crimes: Bluebeard," also printed in October. It was the first in a series by Quinn that ran through November 1924.

Besides the usual pair of reprints and the Lovecraft and Quinn pieces, the seventh *Weird Tales* had thirteen stories, a reprint of Edgar Allan Poe's "The Pit and the Pendulum," "The Eyrie," Quinn's article and the final installment of "The Cauldron."

In addition to the Lovecraft story, I have culled from Volume II, Number 3, Frank Owen's ironic short-short, "The Man Who Owned the World," and "An Adventure in the Fourth Dimension," the best of Farnsworth Wright's contributions to *Weird Tales* and one of the relatively few humorous selections ever to appear in the magazine.

The Man Who Owned The World

FRANK OWEN

I met John Rust by chance one evening in a by-street near Greenwich Village.

It was a miserable night, the air was extremely cold, and a choppy wind kept blowing against my face as though resentful of my presence. And now it commenced to rain, not sufficiently heavy to drive one from the street, yet disagreeable enough to make everything clammy and dismal.

But despite the dreariness of the night, I loitered for a moment before a jewelry store window, probably because I simply cannot pass a window containing gems or pottery or old vases without pausing a moment. There was nothing in the window worthy of recounting, just a heterogeneous assortment of cheap rings, bracelets and gaudy beads almost valueless. Nevertheless, I tarried and then it was that someone grabbed me by the arm, and as I turned around, the jewelry window, the storm, the cold, all were forgotten, for I was gazing into the face of John Rust.

He was so thin that the skin of his face seemed drawn over the raw bones without any intervening layer of flesh. His face was absolutely colorless, even his lips were blue-white. He had a straggly beard, yellow and vile-looking. Even without the enormous shapeless mouth and toothless gums, the beard was sufficient to make the face repulsive.

But it was the unnatural, fanatical light in his eyes which impressed itself most clearly on the screen of my memory. It was not human, but a glow such as might appear in the eyes of a maniac or a wild animal. His costume seemed made up of stray bits from the clothes of all the tramps of earth. And yet he carried a cane and kept swinging it about jauntily as though it were a thing of vast importance.

"You call those jewels!" he cried harshly in a voice made of falsetto notes. "Why, those are not even fit to be thrown to the swine which grovel in a thousand pens more than a mile from my castle. Come with me and I will show you gems more wondrous than the

Crown Jewels of Old Russia, more gorgeous than the collection of Cleopatra and more luxurious than the famed necklace of Helen of Troy. After you see my jewels, you will laugh at what is obviously but a collection of baubles."

On the impulse of the moment, I said, "I will go with you, but before we go, I suggest that we have a bite to eat. You look hungry."

He shrugged his shoulders. "This day," he cried, "have I drunk three pearls melted in golden goblets of rarest wine. But if you wish to eat, I will go with you. All the restaurants near here are mine."

So we went to Messimo's Chop House and ate, but what we ate I cannot recall. As we passed out, John Rust grew quite angry because I paid the check.

"That was foolish," he stormed, "for did I not tell you I owned the restaurant? Tonight I want you to be my guest."

He led the way through a labyrinth of alleys and narrow streets.

"I live apart from the howling mobs," he told me, "so that my sleep will not be disturbed. Each morn I am awakened by a lad as lovely as Narcissus who plays an anthem of the Sun on a harp wrought of gold and platinum and set with a hundred and thirty-three pink diamonds. At the top of the harp is a single square blue diamond of forty carats, the finest in the world. It represents the Morning Star. The strings of the harp are the rays of the sun. The pink diamonds represent the individual kingdoms over which I reign."

As he spoke, we came to a hole in the ground, a filthy, ancient cellar. I must confess that I had a twinge of terror as I followed John Rust down a flight of slippery stone steps, more treacherous and steep than the facade of Gibraltar.

Something, I know not what, scampered across my feet and went screeching off into the blackness which engulfed us like the shadows in a tomb of recent death. I could hear John Rust fumbling about, and after an eternity of waiting, he struck a match and lighted a candle. As he did so, he cried:

"Behold, my treasure-chamber!"

By the dim light of the candle which made the silhouette of John Rust dance on the wall like the capering of a fiend, I glanced about me. The cellar was absolutely unfurnished, unless the cobwebs of a century can be classed as drapery. Down the stone steps the night rain dripped monotonously.

"Look!" fairly shrieked John Rust, "look at these diamonds, sapphires, carved jades, rare corals, tourmalines, emeralds and gorgeous lapis lazuli! Has ever mortal man gazed on a finer collection than this? Here is more wealth than even Midas dreamed of. The Gaekwar of Baroda by comparison to me is without jewels; the Dalai Llama of Tibet is a pauper when the light of my wealth shines upon him. All the treasures of Rome are insignificant when held parallel to mine. The Incas of Peru owned less than I divide in a single year among the poor!"

He clutched at the bits of ashes, coal and pebbles which were falling through his fingers, the wealth which the Gods had lavished on him so prodigiously.

"Tell me," he cried hoarsely, "are your eyes not blinded by the brilliance of my stones?"

"My surprise at what you tell me is acute," I declared truthfully. "I can scarcely find words to express my thoughts."

"Don't try," said John Rust grandly. "The greatest rhetoricians the world has ever known have never invented words even to suggest their true magnificence. . . . Nor is this treasure all I possess. I *own* the world! Every castle of Rome or Venice is mine; every pasture of England, every moor of Scotland, every city in America, I own. Come," he ended abruptly, "come with me, and I will show you my private bath, a pool such as Mark Antony or the mighty Caesar never dreamed of."

It must be confessed that I sighed with relief as he led the way up the worn stone steps again. It was good to be out in the open air once more, even though it was raining as heavily as when Noah set sail.

John Rust led the way back to Washington Square, to the fountain in the center of the park.

"This," he explained, "is my bath, shaded by myrtle trees and palms and in the heart of a grove where ten thousand song birds sing. Among the seven wonders of the world is nothing to equal this. I am better than Monte Cristo, for whereas he only boasted when he exclaimed, 'The world is mine!' I can *prove* my claim to it."

During the days that followed, I met John Rust several times, and although I cannot say that he remembered me, he nevertheless talked to me, which was really all he desired. He believed that all the people in the great city were his slaves and this misconception was the direct cause of his undoing.

While his eccentricities flowed in a harmless channel, he was unmolested, but one day he struck one of his subjects with his scepter. The scepter was a strong oak cudgel and the subject in question was a huge, stalwart ice-man who strenuously objected to being disciplined. He raised such a din that two policemen were necessary to quell his personal riot.

After chaos had ended, the ice-man continued on his rounds, but John Rust was detained until the police-patrol arrived. He believed it was a chariot of gold, that the crowd gathered around had come to envy Caesar, and so he climbed in as majestically as though he were about to proceed to the Coliseum as the supreme guest of the populace on a fete day.

In the course of weeks, a great brain specialist, because he was interested in the case, examined John Rust and asserted that he could be successfully normalized by a simple operation. He went on to explain about the pressure of a bone on some vital spot in the brain, the removal of which would insure the return of rationality.

The operation was successfully performed and eventually John Rust was turned out of the hospital a withered, broken old man, entirely cured.

He went back to his cellar. The first thing he intended doing was to sell his jewels and deposit the money in a reliable bank, for he still retained the memory of his jewels, although the hallucination that he owned the world was entirely blotted out of his memory.

So he returned to his cellar only to find heaps of worthless stones and ashes. He shrieked in his anguish. He had been robbed of all his jewels! For a moment it seemed doubtful that his new-found sanity could stand the surging flood of his ravings. All his enormous wealth had vanished like the essence of a dream. Now life contained nothing for him. He had neither relatives nor friends. He had lived in his dungeon for more than ten years. No one knew from whence he had come. For hours he sat, perhaps even days, moaning and wailing as awfully as any woman for a lost child.

Months later, they found him dead one morning in his cellar, lying face downward in his ashes. He had died of grief, in abject poverty, this man who once had owned the world and had ten million slaves.

An Adventure in the Fourth Dimension

FARNSWORTH WRIGHT

The thought of meteors terrifies me. They have a disagreeable habit of coming down and killing people at the most inopportune times. That is why I was so startled when I saw a large object hurtling toward me out of the sky, as I was walking along the lake front recently in my city of Chicago.

I shivered. Was this the end? I began to say my prayers. To my astonishment, the onrushing missile struck the grass beside me without the slightest jar.

I gasped.

Thousands of singular objects began to detach themselves. They bounded from the mass, and suddenly increased in size from one inch to three feet in diameter. They were entirely round, and covered with teeth. On each tooth were ten ears, constantly in motion. Each ear carried a quizzical eye.

The dwarfish creatures rolled rapidly on the ground, the ears serving as legs, hands, tentacles and what not, propelling them with incredible speed. Sometimes they stood on only four of five of their ears, then suddenly pressed hard against the ground with half a thousand ears at once, thus bounding high into the air. They lit without jar, for the ears acted as shock absorbers and broke their fall.

"Surely these are explorers from Mars or Venus," I thought, as the funny bounding creatures filled the air.

"You are wrong. They are Jupiterians," said a voice beside me.

I recognized the voice. It was Professor Nutt. You probably know him.

"Ahem," he said. "Ahem, ahem!" And once more he repeated, "Ahem!"

"Interesting, if true," I remarked. "And what might Jupiterians be?"

"They might be men, but they're not," he snapped. "They are people from the planet Jupiter. Out of your ignorance you thought they might be Martians or Venusians, but you are wrong, for Mars and Venus have people of three dimensions, like ourselves.

Jupiterians are entirely different. There are six hundred thousand of them in this Jupiterian airship."

I was so overjoyed at finding someone who could tell me about them, that I didn't think to ask him how he knew all these startling facts.

"Where is the airship you speak of?" I asked.

"There it is," he answered, rather grandiloquently, and pointed to an empty spot on the grass.

I looked carefully, and made out a vast, transparent globe, apparently of glass, which was rapidly becoming visible because of the Chicago dust that was settling upon it. I approached, and touched it with my hand. It gave forth a metallic ring.

"Aha!" laughed the professor. "You thought it was glass, but it is made of Jupiterian steel. Look out!"

I sprang back at his warning, and the last hundred thousand leapt out of the globe, passing right through the transparent metal of which it was composed.

"Nom de mademoiselle!" I exclaimed, in astonishment. This was a swear word I had learned in France when I was in the army.

"Nom de mademoiselle!" I repeated, for I liked to show off my knowledge of the language. "How can they pass through the glass without breaking it?"

"Through Jupiterian steel, you mean," said Professor Nutt, severely. "I told you before that it is not glass. Jupiterian steel has four dimensions, and they pass through the fourth dimension. That is why you can't see the metal, for your eyes are only three-dimensional."

"Are the Jupiterian people four-dimensional?" I asked, awed.

"Certainly," said Nutt, rather irritably.

"Then how is it that I can see them?" I exclaimed triumphantly.

"You see only three of their four dimensions," he replied. "The other one is inside."

I turned to look again at the Jupiterians, who now covered the whole waterfront. One of them sprang lightly, fifty feet into the air, extended a hundred ears like tentacles, and seized an English sparrow. He crushed the sparrow with some score or more of his teeth, which, as I have said, covered his whole body. In less than a minute the poor bird was chewed to pieces. I looked closer, and saw that the Jupiterian had no mouth.

"Nom de mademoiselle!" I exclaimed, for the third time. "How can it get the bird into its stomach?"

"Through the fourth dimension," said Professor Nutt.

It was true. The chewed up pieces of the bird were suddenly tossed into the air, and the Jupiterian sprang lightly after them. In mid-air he turned inside out, caught the pieces of the bird in his stomach, and lit on the grass again right side up with care.

"Did you see that?" I exclaimed, in a hushed voice. "Why can't I turn inside out that way?"

"Because you are not four-dimensional," replied the professor, a trace of annoyance in his voice. "It is a beautiful thing to have four dimensions," he rhapsodized. "Your Jupiterian is your only true intellectual, for he alone can truly reflect. He turns his gaze in upon himself."

"And sees what he had for breakfast?" I gasped. "And what his neighbors had, too?"

"Your questions are childish." said the professor, wearily. "A Jupiterian, of course, can look into the soul of things, and see what his neighbors had for breakfast, as you so vulgarly express it. But Jupiterians turn their thoughts to higher things."

The creatures now surrounded me, their ears turned inward, as if they were supplicating.

"What do they want?" I asked the professor.

"They want something to drink," he replied. "They are pointing their ears toward their stomachs to show that they are thirsty."

"Oh," I said, and pointed toward the lake. "There is the fresh, cool water of the lake, if they are thirsty."

"Don't be fantastic," said Professor Nutt. "It isn't water they want."

He fixed his stern, pitiless gaze on my hip pocket. I turned pale, for it was my last pint. But I had to submit. If you ever have had Professor Nutt's cold, accusing eyes on you, you will know just how I felt.

I drew the flask from my pocket, and handed it to the chief Jupiterian, who waggled his ears in joy. Immediately there was pandemonium, if you know what I mean. Ten thousand times ten thousand ears seized the cork, and pulled it out with a resounding pop. One thirsty Jupiterian passed right through the glass into the bottle in his eagerness to get at the contents, and nearly drowned for his pains.

"You see how useful it is to be four-dimensional," remarked the professor. "You could get into any cellar in the world by merely passing through the walls. And into any beer-keg in the same way." "But," I argued, "how did this—this insect get through the glass into the whisky bottle? Glass has only three dimensions, like everything else in this world."

"Don't call him an insect!" Nutt sharply reprimanded me. "He is a Jupiterian, and as such he is infinitely superior to you and me. He passed through the glass because he is four-dimensional, even though the glass isn't. If you had four dimensions, you could untie any knot by merely passing through it yourself. You could turn inside out, or pass through yourself until your right hand became your left hand, and change into your own image as you see it in the looking-glass."

"Nom de mademoiselle!" I exclaimed, for the fourth time.

A distant noise of barking was borne to my ears in the breeze. All the dogs in the city seemed to have gone wild.

"They are disturbed by the talking of the Jupiterians," explained the professor. "It is too high-pitched for clodhopper human ears to hear, unless they have an unusual range, but the dogs can hear it plainly."

I listened, and finally made out a very shrill humming, higher than any sound I had ever heard before in my life, and infinitely sweet and piercing.

"Ah, I am hearing four-dimensional sounds," I thought aloud.

"Wrong, as usual," exacerbated the professor, with much heat. "Sound has no dimensions. It proceeds in waves, and bends back upon itself until it meets itself at an infinite distance from the starting-point. There are three reasons why you can't hear the music of the spheres: first because it is bent away from the earth by the force of gravity as it passes the sun; second, because your ears are not attuned to so shrill a sound; and third, because there is no music of the spheres. The first two reasons are really unnecessary, in the light of the third, but a scientific mind such as mine is not content with one reason when three can be adduced just as easily."

"Shades of Sir Oliver Lodge!" I ejaculated.

"Sir Oliver is alive," the professor corrected me. "A man does not become a shade until after his death. Then he becomes a four-dimensional creature like the Jupiterians, only different."

"Nom de mademoiselle!" I commented.

"Say something sensible." he reprimanded me.

"For the love of Einstein, how do you know all these things about the Jupiterians?" I asked, a sudden suspicion flashing across what I am pleased to call my mind.

"Ah, Einstein, yes," exclaimed Nutt, greatly pleased. "My mother's father's name was Einstein.

"Then you are related to —"

"No, I am not related," he interrupted, "but my mother's father is."

"A sort of fourth-dimensional relationship, I suppose," I remarked sarcastically.

At that moment the air became vibrant with an invisible sound. The Jupiterians came rolling from all directions, as if they had suddenly heard the dinner bell. They bounded through the Jupiterian steel of the globe, and immediately shrank in size from three feet to one inch.

"The Jupiterian assembly call just blew." explained the professor. "Notice how the passengers draw into themselves. Six hundred thousand are now packed into that globe. Our elevated railroads miss a great opportunity by not having four-dimensional creatures to deal with."

"They pack us in just as tight," I ventured to remark.

The globe had begun to shoot into the air, when there came from behind me a high-pitched wail of distress—a shriller and higher sound than had ever before been heard by human ears, so the professor assured me. The chief Jupiterian had been left behind. He it was who had passed into the whisky bottle. Not content with getting the lion's share of the contents, he had surrounded the bottle, in his pleasant four-dimensional way, and now he could not get rid of it.

"Why doesn't he turn inside out again, and drop the bottle?" I asked, watching the Jupiterian with interest.

"Because your whisky has paralyzed him," answered the professor. "He is quite helpless."

I looked at the globe, which had alighted again. Each Jupiterian suddenly resumed his full size, in a brave attempt to bound to the assistance of his chief. But the creatures could no longer pass through the four-dimensional metal of which the globe was composed. So thick a layer of Chicago dust had settled upon it, that to all intents and purposes it had become three-dimensional. The sudden impact of six hundred thousand bodies caused it to burst, with a roar as of a hundred peals of thunder exploding simultaneously. The air was filled with dead and dying Jupiterians. A dark cloud, composed of the flying dust shaken from the Jupiterian globe by the explosion, settled over the landscape. Long streamers of electric fire shot the fragments of the airship, and seemed to curve in upon themselves. Everything ran in curves—the darkness, the cloud, the sounds, the shafts of light—as if bent in by the force of gravity.

I put up my hands and fought the cloud that was settling down upon me. I seemed to be covered with falling feathers, when the cloud began to lift. I found myself in my own parlor. The air was full of flying leaves, which I was madly tearing from a book and throwing toward the ceiling. The book was a treatise on the Einstein theory of space, which I had borrowed from a friend that afternoon. I had read nearly a page in it before I fell asleep.

Only twelve men in the whole world understand the Einstein theory, it is said. If I had read the book, I should have been the thirteenth, and that would be unlucky. So it is just as well that it is destroyed. But what excuse am I to give my friend for tearing up his book?

Dagon

H. P. LOVECRAFT

I am writing this under an appreciable mental strain, since by tonight I shall be no more. Penniless, and at the end of my supply of the drug which alone makes life endurable, I can bear the torture no longer; and shall cast myself from this garret window into the squalid street below. Do not think from my slavery to morphine that I am a weakling or a degenerate. When you have read these hastily scrawled pages you may guess, though never fully realize, why it is that I must have forgetfulness or death.

It was in one of the most open and least frequented parts of the broad Pacific that the packet of which I was supercargo fell a victim to the German sea-raider. The great war was then at its very beginning, and the ocean forces of the Hun had not completely sunk to their later degradation; so that our vessel was made a legitimate prize, whilst we of her crew were treated with all the fairness and consideration due us as naval prisoners. So liberal, indeed, was the discipline of our captors, that five days after we were; taken, I managed to escape alone in a small boat with water and provisions for a good length of time." When I finally found myself adrift and free, I had but little idea of my surroundings. Never a competent navigator, I could only guess vaguely by the sun and stars that I was somewhat south of the equator. Of the longitude I knew nothing, and no island or coast-line was in sight. The weather kept fair, and for uncounted days I drifted aimlessly beneath the scorching sun, waiting either for some passing ship, or to be cast on the shores of some habitable land. But neither ship nor land appeared, and I began to despair in my solitude upon the heaving vastnesses of unbroken blue.

The change happened whilst I slept. Its details I shall never know; for my slumber, though troubled and dream-infested, was continuous. When at last I awaked, it was to discover myself half sucked into a slimy expanse of hellish black mire which extended about me in monotonous undulations as far as I could see, and in which my boat lay grounded some distance away.

Though one might well imagine that my first sensation would be of wonder at so prodigious and unexpected a transformation of scenery, I was in reality more horrified than astonished; for there was in the air and in the rotting soil a sinister quality which chilled me to the very core. The region was putrid with the carcasses of decaying fish, and of other less describable things which I saw protruding from the nasty mud of the unending plain. Perhaps I should not hope to convey in mere words the unutterable hideousness that can dwell in absolute silence and barren immensity. There was nothing within hearing, and nothing in sight save a vast reach of black slime; yet the very completeness of the stillness and the homogeneity of the landscape oppressed one with a nauseating fear.

The sun was blazing down from a sky which seemed to me almost black in its cloudless cruelty; as though reflecting the inky marsh beneath my feet. As I crawled into the stranded boat I realized that only one theory could explain my position. Through some unprecedented volcanic upheaval, a portion of the ocean floor must have been thrown to the surface, exposing regions which for innumerable millions of years had lain hidden under unfathomable Watery depths. So great was the extent of the new land which had risen beneath me, that I could not detect the faintest noise of the surging ocean, strain my ears as I might. Nor were there any seafowl to prey upon the dead things.

For several hours I sat thinking or brooding in the boat, which lay upon its side and afforded a slight shade as the sun moved across the heavens. As the day progressed, the ground lost some of its stickiness and seemed likely to dry sufficiently for travelling purposes in a short time. That night I slept but little, and the next day 1 made for myself a pack containing food and water, preparatory to an overland journey in search of the vanished sea and possible rescue.

On the third morning I found the soil dry enough to walk upon with ease. The odour of the fish was maddening; but I was too much concerned with graver things to mind so slight an evil, and set out boldly for an unknown goal. All day I forged steadily westward, guided by a far-away hummock which rose higher than any other elevation on the rolling desert. That night I encamped, and on the following day still travelled toward the hummock, though that object seemed scarcely nearer than when I had first espied it. By the fourth evening I attained the base of the mound, which turned out to be much higher than it had appeared from a distance; an intervening valley setting it out in sharper relief from the general surface. Too weary to ascend, I slept in the shadow of the hill.

I know not why my dreams were so wild that night; but ere the waning and fantastically gibbous moon had risen far above the eastern plain, I was awake in a cold perspiration, determined to sleep no more. Such visions as I had experienced were too much for me to endure again. And in the glow of the moon I saw how unwise I had been to travel by day. Without the glare of the parching sun, my journey would have cost me less energy; indeed, I now felt quite able to perform the ascent which had deterred me at sunset. Picking up my pack, I started for the crest of the eminence.

I have said that the unbroken monotony of the rolling plain was a source of vague horror to me; but I think my horror was greater when I gained the summit of the mound and looked down the other side into an immeasurable pit or canyon, whose black recesses the moon had not yet soared high enough to illumine. I felt myself on the edge of the world; peering over the rim into a fathomless chaos of eternal night. Through my terror ran curious reminiscences of *Paradise Lost*, and of Satan's hideous climb through the unfashioned realms of darkness.

As the moon climbed higher in the sky, I began to see that the slopes of the valley were not quite so perpendicular as I had imagined. Ledges and outcroppings of rock afforded fairly easy footholds for a descent, whilst after a drop of a few hundred feet, the declivity became very gradual. Urged on by an impulse which I cannot definitely analyze, I scrambled with difficulty down the rocks and stood on the gentler slope beneath, gazing into the Stygian deeps where no light had yet penetrated.

All at once my attention was captured by a vast and singular object on the opposite slope, which rose steeply about an hundred yards ahead of me; an object that gleamed whitely in the newly bestowed rays of the ascending moon. That it was merely a gigantic piece of stone, I soon assured myself; but I was conscious of a distinct impression that its contour and position were not altogether the work of Nature. A closer scrutiny filled me with sensations I cannot express; for despite its enormous magnitude, and its position in an abyss which had yawned at the bottom of the sea since the world was young, I perceived beyond a doubt that the strange object was a well-shaped monolith whose massive bulk had known the workmanship and perhaps the worship of living and thinking creatures.

Dazed and frightened, yet not without a certain thrill of the scientist's or archaeologist's delight, I examined my surroundings more closely. The moon, now near the zenith, shone weirdly and vividly above the towering steeps that hemmed in the chasm , and revealed the fact that a far-flung body of water flowed at the bottom, winding out of sight in both directions, and almost lapping my feet as I stood on the slope. Across the chasm, the wavelets washed the base of the Cyclopean monolith; on whose surface I could now trace both inscriptions and crude sculptures. The writing was in a system of hieroglyphics unknown to me, and unlike anything I had ever seen in books; consisting for the most part of conventionalized aquatic symbols such as fishes, eels, octopi, crustaceans, molluscs, whales, and the like. Several characters obviously represented marine things which are unknown to the modern world, but whose decomposing forms I had observed on the ocean-risen plain.

It was the pictorial carving, however, that did most to hold me spellbound. Plainly visible across the intervening water on account of their enormous size, were an array of bas-reliefs whose subjects would have excited the envy of a Dore. I think that these things were supposed to depict men-at least, a certain sort of men; though the creatures were shewn disporting like fishes in the waters of some marine grotto, or paying homage at some monolithic shrine which appeared to be under the waves as well. Of their faces and forms I dare not speak in detail; for the mere remembrance makes me grow faint. Grotesque beyond the imagination of a Poe or a Bulwer, they were damnably human in general outline despite webbed hands and feet, shockingly wide and flabby lips, glassy, bulging eyes, and other features less pleasant to recall. Curiously enough, they seemed to have been chiselled badly out of proportion with their scenic back-ground; for one of the creatures was shewn in the act of killing a whale represented as but little larger than himself. I remarked, as I say, their grotesqueness and strange size; but in a moment decided that they were merely the imaginary gods of s

one primitive fishing or seafaring tribe; some tribe whose last descendant had perished eras before the first ancestor of the Piltdown or Neanderthal Man was born. Awestruck at this unexpected glimpse into a past beyond the conception of the most daring anthropologist, I stood musing whilst the moon cast queer reflections on the silent channel before me.

Then suddenly I saw it. With only a slight churning to mark its rise to the surface, the thing slid into view above the dark waters. Vast, Polyphemus-like, and loathsome, it darted like a stupendous monster of nightmares to the monolith, about which it flung its gigantic scaly arms, the while it bowed its hideous head and gave vent to certain measured sounds. I think I went mad then.

Of my frantic ascent of the slope and cliff, and of my delirious journey back to the stranded boat, I remember little. I believe I sang a great deal, and laughed oddly when I was unable to sing. I have indistinct recollections of a great storm some time after I reached the boat; at any rate, I know that I heard peals of thunder and other tones which Nature utters only in her wildest moods.

When I came out of the shadows I was in a San Francisco hospital; brought thither by the captain of the American ship which had picked up my boat in mid-ocean. In my delirium I had said much, but found that my words had been given scant attention. Of any land upheaval in the Pacific, my rescuers knew nothing; nor did I deem it necessary to insist upon a thing which I knew they could not believe. Once I sought out a celebrated ethnologist, and amused him with peculiar questions regarding the ancient Philistine legend of Dagon, the Fish-God; but soon perceiving that he was hopelessly conventional, I did not press my inquiries.

It is at night, especially when the moon is gibbous and waning, that I see the thing. I tried morphine; but the drug has given only transient surcease, and has drawn me into its clutches as a hopeless slave. So now I am to end it all, having written a full account for the information or the contemptuous amusement of my fellow-men. Often I ask myself if it could not all have been a pure phantasm-a mere freak of fever as I lay sun-stricken and raving in the open boat after my escape from the German man-of-war. This I ask myself, but ever does there come before me a hideously vivid vision in reply. I cannot think of the deep sea without shuddering at the nameless things that may at this very moment be crawling and floundering on its slimy bed, worshipping their ancient stone idols and carving their own detestable likenesses on submarine obelisks of water-soaked granite. I dream of a day when they may rise above the billows to drag down in their reeking talons the remnants of puny, war-exhausted mankind-of a day when the land shall sink, and the dark ocean floor shall ascend amidst universal pandemonium.

The end is near. I hear a noise at the door, as of some immense slippery body lumbering against it. It shall not find me. God, *that hand!* The window! The window!

NOVEMBER

Volume II, Number 4 was the last *Weird Tales* published in 1923; financial difficulties presumably precluded the December issue. November's sixteen stories, including two by Farnsworth Wright and J. Paul Suter, were notably inferior. The reprint was Edgar Allan Poe's "The Tell-Tale Heart" and the new serial, John Martin Leahy's "Draconda," was noteworthy to the extent that it was the first of six, instead of the usual two, installments. The eighth *Weird Tales* also included "The Grave Robbers," Seabury Quinn's second Weird Crimes article.

My nomination for the issue's best story is "Lucifer," a diabolic "conte cruelle" by John D. Swain.

LUCIFER

JOHN D. SWAIN

The notorious Remsen Case was table talk a year or so ago, although a few today could quote the details offhand. Because of it, half a dozen men were discussing psychic trivialities, in a more or less desultory way. Bliven, the psychoanalyst, was speaking.

"It all hinges on a tendency which is perhaps best expressed in such old saws as: 'Drowning men clutch at straws,' 'Any port in a storm,' or, 'A gambling chance.'

"When men have exhausted science and religion, they turn to mediums, and crystal-gazers, and clairvoyants, and patent medicines. I knew an intelligent pharmacist who was dying of a malignant disease. Operated on three times. Specialists had given him up. Then he began to take the nostrums and cure-alls on his own shelves, although he knew perfectly well what they contained—or could easily enough have found out. Consulted a lot of herb doctors, and long-haired Indian healers, and advertising specialists."

"And, of course, without result," commented the little English doctor.

"I wouldn't say that," said Bliven. "It kept alive the forlorn spark of hope in his soul. Better than merely folding his hands and waiting for the inevitable! He was just starting in with a miraculous Brazilian root, when he snuffed out. On the whole, he lived happier, and quite possibly longer, because of all the fake remedies and doctors he spent so much money on. It's all in your own mind, you know. Nothing else counts much."

"All fakes, including the records of the P.S.R.," nodded Holmes, who lectured on experimental psychology.

The little doctor shook his head depreciatingly.

"I shouldn't go as far as that, really," he objected, "because, every now and then, in the midst of their conscious faking, as you call it, with the marked cards and prepared slates, the hidden magnets and invisible wires and all, these mediums and pseudo-magicians come up against something that utterly baffles them. I have talked with a well-known prestidigitator who has a standing bet of a hundred guineas that he can duplicate the manifestations of any medium; and yet he states that every now and then he finds himself utterly baffled. He can fake the thing cleverly, you understand; but he cannot fathom the unknown forces back of it all. It is dangerous ground. It is sometimes blasphemy! It is blundering in where angels fear to tread."

"Piffle!" snorted Bliven. "The subconscious mind explains it all; and we have only skirted the edge of our subject. When we have mastered it, we shall do thing right in the laboratory that will put every astrologer and palmist and tea-ground prophet out of business."

Nobody seemed to have anything to answer, and the psychoanalyst turned to the little doctor.

"You know this, Royce," he asserted, a bit defiantly.

"I don't pretend to follow you new-era chaps as closely as I ought; but I recall an incident in my early practice that is not explicable in the present-day stage of your science, as I understand it."

Bliven grunted.

"Well—shoot!" he said, "Of course, we can't check up your facts, but if you were an accurate observer, we may be able to offer a plausible theory, at least."

Royce flushed at his brusque way of putting it, but took no offence. Everyone makes allowances for Bliven, who is a good fellow, but crudely sure of himself, and a slave to his hobby.

"It happened a long, long time ago," began Royce, "when I was an interne in a London hospital. If you know anything about our hospitals, you will understand that they are about the last places on earth for anything bizarre to occur in. Everything is frightfully ethical, and prosy, and red-tapey—far more so than in institutions over here, better as these are in many ways.

"But almost anything can happen in London, and does. You love to point to New York as the typical Cosmopolis—because it has a larger Italian population than has Rome, a larger German than Berlin, a Jewish than Jerusalem, and so forth. Well, London has all this, and more. It has nuclei of Afghans, and Turkomans, and Arabs; it has neighborhoods where conversation is carried on in no known tongue. It even has a Synagogue of Negro Jews—dating certainly from the Plantagenet dynasty, and probably earlier.

"Myriads spend all their lives in London, and die knowing nothing about it. Sir Walter Besant devoted twenty years to the collecting of data for his history of the city, and confessed that he had only a smattering of his subject. Men learn some one of its hundred phases passing well; Scotland Yard agents, buyers of old pewter or black-letter books, tea importers, hotel keepers, solicitors, clubmen; but outside of their own little broods the eternal fog, hiding the real London in its sticky, yellow embrace. I was born there, attended its University, practiced for a couple of years in Whitechapel, and migrated to the fashionable Westminster district; but I visit the city as a stranger.

"So, if anything mysterious were to happen anywhere, it might well be in London; although as I have said, one would hardly look for it in one of our solid, dull, intensely prosaic hospitals.

"Watts-Bedloe was the big man in my day. You will find his works in your medical libraries, Bliven; though I dare say he has been thrust aside by the onmarch of science. Osteopathy owes a deal to him, I think; and I know that Doctor Lorenz, the great orthopedist of today, freely acknowledges his own debt.

"There was brought to us one day a peculiarly distressing case; the only child of Sir William Hutchinson, a widower, whose hopes had almost idolatrously centered in this boy, who was a cripple. You would have to be British to understand just how Sir William felt. He was a keen sportsman; played all outdoor games superlatively well, rode to hounds over his own fields, shot tigers from an elephant's back in India, and on foot in Africa, rented a salmon stream in Norway, captained the All-English polo team for years, sailed his own yacht, bred his own hunters, had climbed all the more difficult Swiss peaks, and was the first amateur to operate a biplane.

"So that to natural parental grief was added the bitter downfall of all the plans he had for this boy; instructing him in the fine art of fly-casting, straight shooting, hard riding, and all that sort of thing. Instead of a companion who could take up the life of his advancing years were forcing him to relinquish, in a measure, he had a hopeless cripple to carry on, and end his line.

"He was a dear, patient little lad, with the most beautiful head, and great, intelligent eyes; but his wretched little body was enough to wring your heart. Twisted, warped, shriveled—and far beyond the skill of Watts-Bedloe himself, who had been Sir William's last resort. When he sadly confessed that there was nothing he could do, that science and skillful nursing might add a few years to the mere existence of the little martyr, you will understand that his father came to that pass which you, Bliven, have illustrated in citing the case of the pharmacist. He was, in short, ready to try anything: to turn to quacks, necromancers, to Satan himself, if his son might be made whole!

"Oh, naturally he had sought the aid of religion. Noted clergy of his own faith had anointed the brave eyes, the patient lips, the crooked limbs, and prayed that God might work a miracle. But none was vouchsafed. I haven't the least idea who it was that suggested the to Luciferians to Sir William."

"Luciferians? Devil worshipers?" interrupted Holmes. "Were there any of them in your time?"

"There are plenty of them today; but it is the most secret sect in the world. Huysmand in La-Bas has told us as much as has anyone; and you know perfectly well, or should, that all priests who believe in the Real Presence, take the utmost care that the sacred wafer does not pass into irresponsible hands. Many will not even place it on the communicant's palm; but only in his mouth. For the stolen Host is essential to the celebration of the infamous Black Mass which forms the chief ceremony of the Luciferian ritual. And every year a number of thefts, or attempted thefts, from the tabernaculum, are reported in the press.

"Now the theory of this strange sect is not without a certain distorted rationality. They argue that Lucifer's Star of the Morning, was cast out of Heaven after a great battle, in which he was defected to be sure, but not destroyed, nor even crippled. Today, after centuries of missionary zeal, Christianity has gathered only a tithe of the people into its fold; the great majority is, and always has been, outside. The wicked flourish, often the righteous stumble; and at the last great battle of Armageddon, the Luciferians believe that their champion will finally triumph.

"Meanwhile, and in almost impenetrable secrecy, they practice their infamous rites and serve the devil, foregathering preferably in some abandoned church, which has an altar, and above it a crucifix, which they reverse. It is believed that they number hundreds of thousands, and flourish in every quarter of the world; and it is presumed that they employ grips and passwords. But amid so much that is conjecture, this fact stands clear: the cult of Lucifer does exist, and has from time immemorial.

"I never had the least idea who suggested them to Sir William. May have been some friend who was a secret devotee, and wished to make a proselyte. Nay have been an idle word overheard in a club—or penny bus. The point is, he did hear, discovered that an occult power was claimed by their unholy priests, was ready to mortgage his estate or sell his soul for this little chap, and somehow got in touch with them.

"The fact that he managed it, that he browbeat Watts-Bedloe into permitting one of the fraternity to enter the hospital at all, is the best example I an give of his despairing persistence. At that, the physician agreed only upon certain seemingly prohibitive conditions. The fellow was not to touch the little patient, nor even to draw near his bed. He was not to speak to him, or seek to hold his gaze. No phony hypnotism, or anything like that.

"Watts-Bedloe, I think, framed the conditions in the confident hope that they would end negotiations; and he was profoundly disgusted when he learned that the Luciferian, though apathetic, was not in the least deterred by the hardness of the terms. It appeared that he had not been at all willing to come under any circumstances; that he tried persistently to learn how Sir William had heard of him, and his address, and that he had refused remuneration of any sort. Altogether, a new breed of fakir, you see!

"There were five of us in the room at the time appointed, besides the little patient, who was sleeping peacefully. Fact is, Watts-Bedloe had taken the precaution of administering a sleeping draught, in order that the quack might not in any possible way work upon his nervous system. Watts-Bedloe was standing by the cot, his sandy hair rumpled, his stiff moustache bristling, for all the world like an Airdale terrier on guard. The father was there, of course; and the head nurse, and a powerful and taciturn orderly. You can see that there wasn't much chance of the devil-man pulling off anything untoward!

"When, precisely on the moment, the door opened and he stood before us, I suffered as great a shock of surprise as ever in my life; and a rapid glance at my companions' faces showed me that their amazement equaled mine. I don't know just what type we had visualized—whether a white-bearded mystic clad in a long cloak with a peaked hat bearing cabalistic symbols, or a pale, sinister and debonair man of the world, such as George Arliss has given us, or what not; but certainly not the utterly insignificant creature who bowed awkwardly, and stood twirling a bowler hat in his hands as the door closed behind him.

"He was a little, plump, bald man of middle age, looking for all the world like an unsuccessful greengrocer, or a dealer in butter and cheese in a small way. Although the day was cool, with a damp yellow fog swirling over the city, he perspired freely, and continually wiped his brow with a cheap bandana. He seemed at once ill at ease, yet perfectly confident, if you know what I mean. I realize that it sounds like silly rot; but that is the only way I can describe him. Utterly certain that he could do that for which he had come, but very much wishing that he were anywhere else. I heard Watts-Bedloe mutter 'my word!' And I believe he would have spat disgustedly—were such an act thinkable of a physician in a London hospital!

"The Luciferian priest turned to Sir William. When he spoke, it seemed entirely in keeping with his appearance that he should take liberties with his aspirates. 'I'm 'ere, m'lord. And h'at your service.'

"Watts-Bedloe spoke sharply, 'Look here, my man!' he said. 'Do you pretend to say that you can make this crippled child whole?'

"The strange man turned his moist, pasty face, livid in the fog murk, toward the specialist. 'E that I serves can, and will. I'm a middleman, in a manner of speaking. A transmitter. H'its easy enough for 'im, but I don't advise it, and I warns you I'm not to be 'eld responsible for 'ow 'E does it.'

"Watts-Bedloe turned to Sir William. 'Let's have an end to the sickening farce,' he said curtly. 'I need fresh air!'

"Sir William nodded to the little man, who mopped his brow with his bandana, and pointed to the cot. 'Draw back the coverlet!' he commanded.

"The nurse obeyed, after a questioning glance at Watts-Bedloe. 'Tyke off 'is night gown,' continued the visitor.

"Watts-Bedloe's lips parted in a snarl at this, but Sir William arrested him with a gesture, stepped to his son's side, and with infinite gentleness took off the tiny gown, leaving the sleeping child naked in his bed.

"Again, as always, I felt a surge of pity sweep through me. The noble head, the pigeon breast, rising and falling softly now, the crooked spine, the little gnarled, twisted limbs! But my attention was quickly drawn back to the strange man.

"Barely glancing at the child, he fumbled at his greasy waistcoat, Watts-Bedloe watching him meanwhile like a lynx, as he took out a crumb of chalk and, squatting down, drew a rude circle on the floor about him; a circle of possibly four feet in diameter. And within this circle he began laboriously to write certain worked and figures."

"Hold on there!" spoke Bliven. "Certain words and figures? Just what symbols, please?"

"There was a swastika emblem," Royce promptly replied, "and others familiar to some of the older secret orders, and sometimes found on Aztec ruins and Babylonian brick tablets; the open eye, for instance, and a rude fist with thumb extended. Also he scrawled the sequence 1-2-3-4-5-6-7-9, the '8' omitted, you notice, which he multiplied by 18, and again by 27, and by 36; you can amuse yourselves working it out. The result is curious. Lastly, he wrote the sentence, 'Sigma te, sigma, temere me tangis et angis.' A palindrome, you observe; that is, it reads equally well—or ill, backward or forward."

"Hocus pocus! Old stuff!" snorted Bliven.

Royce gazed mildly at him.

"Old stuff, as you say, professor. Older than recorded history. Having done this, a matter of five minutes, perhaps, with Watts-Bedloe becoming more and more restless, and evidently holding himself in with difficulty, the fellow rose stiffly from his squatting position, carefully replaced the fragment of chalk in his pocket, mopped his brow for the twentieth time, and gestured toward the cot with a moist palm. 'Now, cover 'im h'up!' he ordered. 'All h'up; 'ead and all.'

"The nurse gently drew the sheet over the little form. We could see it rise and fall with the regular respiration of slumber. Suddenly, eyes wide open and staring at the floor, the fellow began to pray, in Latin. And whatever his English, his Latin was beautiful to listen to, and virgin pure! It was too voluble for me to follow verbatim—I made as good a transcript as I could a bit later, and will be glad to show it to you, Bliven—but, anyhow, it was a prayer to Lucifer, at once an adoration and a petition, that he would vouchsafe before these Christian unbelievers a proof of his dominion over fire, earth, air and water. He ceased abruptly as he had begun, and nodded toward the cot. 'H'it is done!' he sighed, and once again mopped his forehead.

" 'You infernal charlatan!' snarled Watts-Bedloe, unable longer to contain himself. 'You've got the effrontery to stand there and tell us anything has been wrought upon that child by your slobbering drivel?'

"The man looked at him with lusterless eyes. 'Look for yerself, guv'ner.' he answered.

"It was Sir William who snatched back the sheet from his son; and till my dying day I shall remember the unearthly beauty of what our astounded eyes beheld. Lying there, smile upon his lips, like a perfect form fresh from the hand of his Creator, his little limbs straight and delicately rounded, a picture of almost awesome loveliness, lay the child we had but five minutes before seen as a wrecked and broken travesty of humanity."

Again Bliven interrupted explosively:

"Oh, I say now, Royce! I'll admit you tell a ripping story, as such; you had even me hanging breathless on your climax. But this is too much! As man to man, you can't sit there and tell us this child was cured!"

"I didn't say that; for he was dead."

Bliven was speechless, for once; but Holmes spoke up in remonstrance:

"It seems strange to me that such a queer story should not have been repeated, and discussed!"

"It isn't strange, if you happen to know anything about London hospitals," Royce explained patiently. "Who would repeat it? Would Watts-Bedloe permit it to be known that by his permission some charlatan was admitted, and that during his devilish incantations his patient died? Would the stricken father mention the subject, even to us? Or the head nurse and orderly, cogs in an inexorable machine?

"All this took place nearly forty years ago; and it is the first time I have spoken of it. Watts-Bedloe died years back; and Sir William's line is extinct. I can't verify a detail; but it all happened exactly as I have stated. As for the Luciferians, none of us, I think, saw him depart. He simply stole out in to the slimy yellow fog, back to whatever private hell it was he came from, somewhere in London, the city nobody knows, and where anything may happen!"

AFTERWORD

The first year of *Weird Tales* contains a few other worthwhile works of fiction that I eventually hope to anthologize. At the top of the list are two more Julian Kilman horror stories, "The Affair of the Man in Scarlet" (April) and "The Mystery of Black Jean" (March), the latter a particularly nasty study in sadism, murder and bestiality. I do not admire Anthony M. Rud's twice-reprinted first *Weird Tales* contribution, "Ooze," but was impressed with his second story, "A Square of Canvas," a savage tale of madness that ran in the April issue and was reprinted in September 1951, as well as in *Weird Tales: 32 Unearthed Terrors*, edited by Stefan R. Dziemianowicz, Robert Weinberg and Martin H. Greenberg (Bonanza Books, 1988).

May includes Vincent Starrett's "Penelope," an odd item about a protagonist temporarily beset by a reverse flow of gravity. (Sam Moskowitz claims Starrett admitted borrowing the idea from a pulp story he'd once read.) Another interesting selection in the May issue is "The Closed Cabinet," an anonymous tale of an English haunting that is either a remarkably excellent pastiche of Victorian prose or a first-rate period piece. Unfortunately, it was much too long (22,000 words) for inclusion in this volume.

Of lesser significance, but still deserving mention are four stories from the first issue—Howard Ellis Davis's "The Unknown Beast," Willard E. Hawkins's "The Dead Man's Tale" (reprinted in July 1934), David R. Solomon's "Fear" and Merlin Moore Taylor's "The Place of Madness"—and one from November 1923, Valens Lapsley's anomalous "The Pebble Prophecy."

Printed in the United States
109731LV00001B/21/A

9 781880 448533